Contents

Journey

Act One

(Saint Martin and Saint John discuss Universal truths, John stage left, Martin stage right, a simple enough instruction for actors to follow. The other character's find their place as instructed with their entrance, within reason to find themselves and express themselves as they seem fit for their part-end of intro)

John: Where ere it's possible to send a soul, where ere its breath leaves trust asunder, there lies the last breath of a man. For want of other places, for escape, for sanctuary for the pain and sufferings of life, there lies the want of this here testing restless place.

Martin: This lies true in pains and pleasures, easy leisure's, trusted things for a soul to do. What appetites lye in wait for this soul or another brings clarity to our most recent and illustrious past, here and now, the great denial, Jacobs Ladder, Purgatory, spirit land, judgement, death of body, it's all over. Been as is and will forever be.

John: It's all over yet it's just beginning too for this here soul. The soul of man, the soul of the one, all are one, now done its true search for dignity is found at last in death, in his last breath, last beat, last gesture. Moreover, the lash is spared from tempestuous temptations lesser souls have chosen. Paupers spirits rule the soul of the damned. How they revel in their appetites. Dirty little Divils.

Martin: Multiplicity and mighty appetites for shame and self-deprivation burned in the pale of valour's demolition. Afterthoughts adjacent vaccinated spirits wrenched outwards in through more unappetising futile futuresque firmaments. Emotionally stunted academic minds, blind bone-headed imbeciles, puppets of someone else's idiotic thoughts.

John: Masters of nothing but the stunting of more artistic green fingered sensitive souls. Foul stenched furnace burns within the bodies strength in roaring fires fortunes spent on appetites indulged. Borders broadened essence embers glowing spires downed for dust and nothingness. Philistine verses angel, all round the earths diagram. Spheres upon spheres.

Martin: Wells the hole divides young sons and daughters from others forgiving embrace. Raging waters wash the poor in spirit from the edges of the earth. Whirlpools bashing bodies on the rocks as slithering monsters' demand their eternal reprimand. One thousand years a poltergeist. One hundred thousand years a ghoul, eternities organic time loop circumnavigates the globe.

John: A fair price for a head no longer worth its weight in gold or silver. An end to debauched poor mouthed ragged raging fools. Schooled by their own wild hypocrisies, broken and bent by the weight of their own worthless lives. I feel a roaring appetite for vengeance and I must avoid the price of victories on common fools. Tapping ever thrice on eternities unpolished, unvarnished doors.

Martin: Its great! Wonderful! All self-inflicted self-absorbed misguided infidels. The battle we place with mortal bodies in this our territory, our well-worn roads between the firmaments, above the divide, through the fires of Sunlight and volcanic molten rivers flow, out in the oceans and deep down within the bowels of the earth's grave caverns.

John: The beasts do roam, the black snake-backed goliaths make little of men and their armies. Make mice of men, make dust of bones and more the sound of moaning can be heard from tired suffering souls at night by the banished subterranean troglodytes ever glowing furnaces. Bright the flame that purifies, great the light that illuminates, throughout the darkness lies hopes twinkling giants. Lost souls weep as Christ leaves them well enough alone. There be a window without light down endless corridor's inescapable.

Martin: Whipped by Demons and imps, tortured by dark wild beasts that roam the minds of men that suck the marrow of their bones. Cruel natured humans carnivorous appetising structures long in their birth by Gods and angels fill the bellies of great dragons unappeased by sinful wickedness and selfish damned imbeciles. They didn't know the price of ignorance, knew nothing of suffering, caused the same, paid measures price. For the love of someone else's lunch money. Metaphors of modernity for modernity, the ever-sickening schoolyard bullies eternal suffering self-inflicted diabolical destiny.

John: Open mindedness expels intellect where mindfulness expels moral thought. Laymen find nothing but hounds in purity. Hell hounds beset upon humanities weaknesses during their obliterations judgement. Over-bearing thoughtlessness eventually leads to lustful appetites and wondrous delights for all the imps of the pit to play great games with the lost souls of humanity. Thrones filled by the bones of their forefathers, bludgeoned gaseous worthless backsides worth nothing to hungry mouths. Stolen years lost for an eternity.

Martin: Dark indeed this time and place where angels and demons spring about with sylphs in atmospheres lost to wandering eyes and loosened gripped realities. Dark entities maraud the minds of peoples lost to lucid atmospheres of inherited confusion and wild weathers bounty.

John: Wandering souls flitter through perditions quagmires of vengeful millennium life like rusted winter leaves that skit through the air, ruined, tattered and torn. Bearing the subterfuge many years of toil, wearily on to rise above it all and outshine the saints of Christianity with good deeds inner peace and fortitude.

6

Ahh, almost too easy right!

Martin: Great news! More power in opposites, more strength in extremes, more money in more from ore and gold, silver and slavery, more business, industry, colonies, infrastructure, segregation Communism, Consumerism, isms for all the family. Where's a mighty humble leader when you need one.

John: Mighty stuff! Scepticism for the masses, that's where the big bucks lye. Movement of collateral from one source to another, voting and choking simultaneously as Christmas celebrations come round again, thank God! Whew! (Both men wipe their foreheads) Perhaps next year well have a real politician who delivers on their words. A soothsayer, a prophet whose soul is true to Celtic lore and law, virtues of the innocent!

Martin: Black and white, day and night, male, female war and peace, write and wrong, silence songs, silenced mouths, stolen children. Highways and byways, bent as Hell or straight as a die, crooked or wrenched from home and country. Compassion cures little for the empty bellies of starving paupers fox cubs. Metaphors do ride the back of leviathans set free on humanities bounteous beating heart.

John: Institutionalised solutions, excommunications for all non-believers, frustrations of indebted nations, king-sized bills, death knell, pounding the flesh, meshed up with the next true-blue git, running rancid the people like blue-arsed flies, time to live, time to die. Moronic imbeciles, voted in by winning wonders. Skin changing anachronised misogynistic misanthropic priests and bishops prophesising Pagan atrocities they themselves have made more of a meal of than any gluttonous cannibalistic infidel found living peacefully in ignorance and bliss.

Martin: Holy God! They have, half of them good though doing nothing. Much like their congregation, where are the lynch mobs, the ignorant villagers fiery torch in hand ousting the virus of evil from their parishes still today running rampant with vile disgusting filth.

John: Half of them evil:

Martin: So it is written.

John: So shall it be. Amen.

Martin: Amen to that! What do the old Gods think of that! What roads have led to modernity's alien culture shock on all of us indeed.

John: Mentally and blindly misguided mothered complex narcissistic bloated bated blithering Neanderthals, lead astray by abusive childhoods, alcoholic parents, demonic possession, thrown to who's to blame, God? The Devil? Mother Teresa? Ghandi, Colonising kings and queens What soldier from his bombed out grave doesn't live in light to oversee the plight his country suffers at the hands of ignorant religious royalty. Non believers only of course, within the sacred satin gowns of the lost souls of self delusion and hypocrisy. Assume the position!

Martin: Sacrilege! Blasphemies! (Points at John) Burn thou in Hell! You foul mouthed pauper, you starving masses, you uncultivated swine! Oh well bred royals with light skin and fair complexion, the beautiful ones, the light of the world, the illuminating godlike creature features richer than Jesus, beaming shallow empty vessels of meaninglessness and a dried up vampiric Satanic mess. The only rich solution is abominable exclusion.

John: Oh wondrous delights for troglodytic sprites here news for you, now's your time to fight for flight against the fallen impervious angels of humanity. Righteous vengeful revenge on the fallen hypocrites who's whole story lies in wait for gentler souls anticipated. Moreover the sounds of truth fall heavy on heads born to rule as the worm beats its fleshy mould upon the brains of youth.

Martin: Mental bacteria, virus, plague and famine rule on modernity's confused state. Bound for eternities diseased minds and twisted thwarted domains. Modern technologies thwarted dualistic forces birthing addictions that in themselves take more life, bring only stolen years to innocence and drive the paths of perdition further still. Ahh, its a grand day....

John: Blessed are the children who see only the light of escape, who find avenues untouched by their failed adversaries. Those that strive for victory over the bent and twisted chemically addicted dogs of Hell. Blessed art those that endure to educate themselves to higher goals, that fire the bound and bleeding wrists of wandering souls.

Martin: Blessed are the hands that wash the skin, that feed the body well and run faster than lycanthropes, for they will have to. That out-think the demon minded idiots, that duel within themselves, that avoid sloth and blame. That bring light to the darkness and falter not at temptations diseased door.

John: Blessed are the young at heart for theirs is the kingdom of truth and leisure. This evenings glorious tide passes on to heated hearths warm, welcoming glowing fires, relaxed after the tempest work days past. Breathing hope into tired souls for a well earned rest from trepidation.

Martin: How poetic he is! (Looks at audience holding right hand out, palm up, then back to normal) Majestic, exquisite perfections completed toil and wondrous delights on the modern equivalent of theatre and spectacle. The recreations pastime for families to chill, upon that reclined throne, their favourite cushioned place.

John: To chill indeed in modernity's and technological wizardries of miraculous invention. For wired bits and bobs, for glass and gold creations filled with magical lights and electrical creation. For this world does indeed reflect the other in its mastery and enigmatic magnificence.

Martin: Well said sir! Has humanity not crawled out from the caves, from the oceans, from millennia of monkey men, lizards and salamanders! Moved away from that cold dark wet and unwelcoming world where animal and man live in proximity to deaths dreary dogmatic rules and regulations, deep within the labyrinth. So they have swapped the cost of invention for the cold wet hard reality of Mother Natures baleful preoccupation with the suffering of man.

John: Its no wonder all this does kill that nature by its own usage. What world is this that cannot leave it well enough alone, the hand of mankind's own pleasures lead to pain. As mother nature intended, all is suffering all is joy, in betweens the Summer months and for to aft a chilling season. Then winter in all its frozen glory rains on children's dreams like a menacing goliath fuelled by rage and terrors unknown to tiny hearts and brains.

Martin : Appetites born of Lycanthropic hungers, brethren of greed, brothers of death and suffering, yet children all the same. Innocence has many forms, modernity is no stranger to the God of slumber, the Concubines of addictions, the masters of addictions. There lies the stub of a smoking gun, made only of paper and dust.

John: Your bouncing off the walls today, God bless you! The medley of mass recreation, that which makes man less human, yet less animal, yet more beast, yet less demon, yet more angel of pleasure and harmonious hedonistic leisure's. A grand time was had by all asunder. A den of delights and iniquity for all and temperance the key.

Martin: What joyous pleasures lye in healthy times. A little bit of this, a little bit of that. Its only an accepted social norm the Gods of pleasure abound in mans need for stress relief. Laws broken but laws allowed lead only to more laws broken. Herein the modern form of Opium, the Goddess Heroic, sleeping dreamer, gentle seductress. Powders of enjoyment, pills for ecstatic experience. A politicians joy.

John: All good for the soul, the lycanthrope says, as it waits for the children of the Divine to slip slowly down into the labyrinth, the paths of their forefathers, where the horned Minotaur awaits. The stories of fallen hero's follow close the bones of relatives. The hero made man, the challenger to evils sticky hidden secrets. The thirst for vengeance held in the hearts of smited victims. Close to the marrow. Merlin's end by poisonous spiders touch. She that cannot abide others.

Martin: Suckling at the side of every sleeping soul, an imp and his master await for the cold hands of death to slip into the heart of man. Monstrous crimes injuries, calamities, appear as ripples in the pond, where once great tsunamis of fault and reprimand obey the chance of pain. Great is the gain, little the reward.

John: Last breaths, fear flourishes where times immeasurable toil strangles all around. Boundless creatures frail to their marrow after lifetimes guzzling liquids maiden pleasures. Livers rot and hearts falter in the hands of well worn luxuries. Endless revelries for the hedonistic soul, the hearty working consumers.

Martin: Monumental irretrievable youth, banished health, fallen angels, eternal hangovers and ritual sufferings. Where no devils are needed, the weight of over indulgence survives in bodies ready for the grave. Marriages burned by sin, by lies, by addictions un-natural. Reputations ruined, agonising internal suffering.

John: Impotence, baldness, fat stomached, weakness in the knees, ugly faced inner horrors, toothless Hell. Debt ridden by drinking all the children's holidays, all the college fees all the new clothes torn. Woeful mysteries. Baleful hypocrites preaching Hellfire needing oceans to extinguish their own internal combustions. Pure unadulterated filth, the lowest form of life.

Martin: (Laughs loud and holds his head back) Woeful mysteries, crossed hearts, full of golden years, wasted in failed health on midlife crisis remedies and broken barbarous banalities. Over indulged stomachs bulging at seamless stretched foul turned moronic imbeciles. More debt for our society.

John: God forgive their failed philosophies, baleful fortunes, broken marriages, bandy legged dreams. Out from the wilderness and down trodden worn out shoes, stinking of booze and tobacco with crooked fingers found unwelcome at every corner. Even well dressed they stand as soul-less corpses bound to wrinkled miseries.

Martin: Sad is the old fool that's forced to seek shelter in the lord after 5o years a drinking, 50 years a smoking, 50 years a cheating, lying, hypocrites without any hope of retirement. There is no God! There's only whoring, snoring, boring pleasures to kill life's pains, to seek solace in idiocy and ignorance. What a shame indeed, the soul of the damned imbecile. Would you sign your name for him and hers?

John: It takes a strong man to laugh at his bodies demise, it takes a stronger man to rid himself of ill health and dreadful reputation. How well do old gossiping devils know well the soul that is freed from addiction and hedonistic pursuits? A soul set free by the charismatic absolution of the divine intervention that rules all life.

Martin: The orbs within the broken souls body know well the power of thought. For its well known in Eastern religions that only those of extreme dysfunction can become absolute masters of the spirit body. Solution extraordinaire! Waaooh! Mighty Aphrodite!

John: The great Siddhartha! Mentor of Christ, foreign God of immense purity once lived as an orgy addicted opium guzzling madman-beatnick! What lies beneath the skin of a sinner will dominate the lives of controlling local deprivation addicts. Smokers of the divine Kali-lost souls soothing themselves in the opiate wells within.

Martin: Though those same gossiping devils prey to the spirit of that saint, whom once sold her body for hedonistic pleasures. The ever decrepit mind of man spends lifetimes thinking of how weak and naive are other people, when those very same people rise above the dogs of the road and shine brighter than Lucifer himself!

John: I too wore the clothes of shame, I too lived as a menacing lycanthrope, marauding at night the imp infested establishments of spirits of high percentage. Roaming after women's beauty, revelling in the chemistries within. The apothecary of adrenalines and serotonins and opium's within the blood. Lost to pleasure and joy, wondrous ways of youthful fearlessness.

Martin: Woeful streams of tears come from vanquished eyes, cries of fear and esoteric moaning deep within the angry soul who's life no longer resembles Christian. Boring on the floor of fate, rolling by the cold fireside of failure lies a man who's very life awaits a measure. Drop after pure drop leads to nothing.

John: Very poetic. Giant arms that suffocate the throat as sinners arms lengths away from deaths carnivorous door handles, loose their grip and cry God! (He bellows towards the audience-as a writer I would like the actor to use method acting here for a time in their life where they couldn't take any more and cried out to God on an absolutely deep level of need) God! They cry holding their hands outstretched, please God, save me! What do you want from me! Why am I dying!

Martin: Who is trying to kill me? Why are they so evil, they are so evil and bitter and controlling! Such an ugly soul, a pig, a fat bullying beast of a pig! I want to kill that person, I want to kill that man. I want to pull the skin off their placid impotent faces and rip it off their skull and pour vinegar into their brain!

John: I want to stab their heads until there's no more head to see. To crunch their bones and feed the to the pigs, to spread their bloodied mess on the streets of shame and cry I win! I beat you! I am stronger! I am the God damned man around here! Not you, you pig scum filth abusive-abused monstrous hag from Satan's rump!

Martin: God forgive your foul mouthed sense of humour brother.

John: God forgive me. (He holds his hands up to the roof closing his eyes)But we have to vent when pushed beyond the boarders of our sanity. Scratch the skin of an Irishman, find a psychopath in waiting.

Martin: What is this cold winter, this iced out freeze of bent and twisted local warriors? Whose war are they fighting? Why must I fight? Who will punish my anger? Cannot I live my life! Cannot I rule my domain? What bloody war is about now in this end of days? What cowards run down the innocent child like weeds on my streets in the light of day?

John: Its an unforgiving world poor soul. The angels forgive us, they know of anger and of shame.

Martin: Poor soul indeed. Yet I have seen many the soul nearer to the end stand up and fight, this way, always this way, the rout of anger, the last bastion of the slothful fool. Roaming through life, the earth for many the year in search of loves sweet comforts, the gentle touch of fate and success, the sounds of angels selling opiates of joy and love. The comforts of recreations dream, the fantasy of escape, the taste of freedoms favourite and consumed.

John: Weekend sin indulgences do indeed lessen the blow of work, of waiting, of want, for the hand that feasts itself cannot want for anything but water in the mourning. For a healthy meal made by mother, a soulful feed of lamb roast and gravy in the hearth where goodness rules and innocence tasted yet again. If only temporarily.

Martin: Mark not evil by the hand of hedonists, more they are gods themselves, gods of generosity, gods of charity and celebration. Ancient gods where all is nothing but experimentational excess in moderation. Yes! Excessive moderation, long is the night, savoured be the choices found, great quality in weed and liquor. Only the best for our children of leisure. Then perdition, the hangover that just doesn't quit.

John: Artists of exploration, hallucinogens make famous men roar the world round. The round table of artistic endeavour, the scream of the butterfly, the howl of the lycanthrope reflects well its opposite angelic chaste counterpart in spirits nature. If you cant do the time, ignore the consequences, stop being a man, lift your arse up to the skies and cry freedom!

Martin: Who's ghost will tell of secret sins, unveiled at times of trial and tribulation. What slight mistakes in drunken slumber lead to judgment as unwelcome advances. As unrequited experiences, any drunken fool can make and forever wonder as to why they did some slight unrequested act. Cry wolf! When in later years it all comes crumbling down upon their heads. Ahh, Thank God for Repentance in repetition, the addicts opinion.

John: The headlessness of hedonistic years comes crawling back from the graves of blacked out memories. Unsure if sin was committed or not. Not all men escape the touch of blame, not all women escape the veil of blame even though its printed in the everyman's papers every day. Poor little Jezebels daughters cannot be held accountable for their drunken mistakes. Lilith cries wolf, when her teeth are laced with the blood of innocents.

Martin: True men must be blamed for all sins in the daily bread of multi media and modern stories for sale on every counter. Men are monsters, women are wonderful, soothsaying goddesses unaccountable for any action, deed or thought, so the saying goes. Those evil sisters of the cloth swiftly forgotten, move on story tellers, its men that are guilty, not the sisters of suffering men of

15

war. God bless the angels of course.

John: Great is the fear of blame on sisters, great all fear the anger of Lilith, Devil bloodthirsty beast of Hell. No wonder mankind shy's from thoughts that evil women wander the globe as much as evil men do. What of the psychological sinner? Cannot they find redemption after suffering, after paying for their crimes? The negative thoughts that eat away at the mind of little children. The eternal harassment by open mouths bent on shaming angels.

Martin: Not in the minds of the masses, all projecting their sins onto those that are caught out, or punished in the wrong. Still many think that one punished by the law must it go unpunished, for the fear the law may come after them, or theirs as it does anyway. Catch twenty two, the mind of the sinner.

John: Roaring down the throats of the masses comes the lycanthropes ever spiralling attack. Ever onwards humanity suffers from panicked mistakes made by forefathers, made both men and by women. Child made monster, victim made monster. Starving pauper made terrorist, child killer, patriot killer, freedom fighter.

Martin: The circus continues, the clowns made joker, the innocent suffer to become the tyrant and all cry victim in between. Sisters of freedom fighters cry victim to bloodied blameless in their tombs. What bloodied corpse is our country now, what world is this? For want of heat, the world is boiled, for want of clothes the cupboards are overflowing, for want of freedom, the hand of man finds more idolatry and less escape from suffering.

John: What jezebel doesn't want to cry wolf! When one drunken Friday night leads to the birth of a death. Small consequence to a countries oaths and laws when fair is fair, unplanned children don't make ife easier, now do they?

Martin: No, oh no they don't, they get in the way of everything, its not fair on them either to be born into a loveless or poverystricen life. Its a tough world after all, who knows what we would do if we where in the same osition. Still screaming victims of oppression cry evil! Let us make our own minds up, its our life after all.

John: Petrhapstrhey should be given the right o suicide, euthanasia at an early age, its their choice isn't it, why not. I know many theman or woman that deserves to leave it all behind. Iiving a painfull horrific existence of abuse and suffering is no oath for a child. Iving in a world full of imbeiclci moronic infidel is no walk in the park either, is it? (He truns to the audience and holds his hands upwards as if asking them)

Martin: More of that does it not pain men to suffer for their crimes, or suffer just because they aremen? How easyit is to think a man as sinner, how easily vilifies are men by all persona. Thick soups of Hell ride on the sholders of alcoholic abusers and their children. The ravens of Death. The all blaming mob of dishevelled trogledites.

John: The throng of lost souls whos destiny lies here on earth in an after-life as ghost stinking breath and unwelcome cold death hands in the beds of innocents. Colege days haunted by poltergeists from early graves, never seeing the light, rejected all messiahs, roaring for the pain and mysery of young gente intelligent middle class pillars of furutr society.

Martin: Ohhorros indeed, woefull insufferable suffering and tendencies for rotten foul stenched evil. Tied to the spot, under the covers washed by their othes, frozen by paralising beasts once man, once woman. Sisters of jezebel that rape the sons of man in his innocence, under the clean sheets his mother gave him.

Jihn: You paint a bleak picture my son. Bleak and weary it isto suffer the soul sucking verin that rule the roost of midnights blue domain. Though I lay me down to sleep, where the hell is the local excorsist when youneed one! Buried in the work of doom, glistening in his solitude. Ah it sounds much better that way, poetic artistry abounds.

Martin: Ever doubtfullmans dominion ever craving scpe from blame, where responsibilities avoided seem less important than the words from mouthes made brainless. So who really cares about some other life lost? Who cares for foreign regulations, where liberties taken rule all hands, all handless stumps. Cut from the arms of thieves right in view of the mobbing publics bulging eyes.

John: The cold world is here in this room, out in the wilderness of the cities neon lights. There in the homestead in the deafened ears of mother. The last hope for a dying soul, the sacred sanctuary of home. The gentle word from mater, a calming reasuriing word of hope for a toiling suffering mess of a fool brought to sedation usually intoxicated temperance follies function.

Martin: Theres a lottosay for the strong hedonistic world weary traveller, they have the strength of survival at their sida. Tarry on and oarry the tests of righteous enemies, many the knight has fallen when his brothers fail him. Mantthe thief survives when the innocent suffer.

John: Ruin and bastardised unions! To war! To waste! To Hell and back I will survive! A rancid scarred heathen God fearing barbarian Celtic, Pagan antichrist am I! I will not die! I will live! I will work somehow they damned souls of this millennium will takeme in somewhere, they must, there must be a solution, I live!

Martin: I'm alive, I live, I survive, I work when they let me. I survive the damned souls of this time, this madhouse of a world full of headless imbeciles and insane characters disgraced at every turn they find. Where's the solace in this time, thank God I have no child, who would want to birth into the pit that is this time? God bless the innocent babes!

John: For those last moments of the dying souls life, those last days of painful bones worn down by lifelessness and worries. The suffering of family arguing and restlessness, vertigo and fear of the future. Pills, pills and more flaming pills! The silent hours alone with no one to share their thoughts with even though they are surrounded by loved ones.

Martin: You paint a bleak picture my friend, indeed but this is also a beginning, the beginning of the giving time. That same soul gives up his struggle to remain his own master and says "God, I give myself to you, I surrender my will, I have lived wrong, done wrong, I have been selfish and followed the path of shallow men. Humanity is resilient, a few good Summers is all it takes to turn things around.

John: Yes, I surrender my will lord to you, that is the real start, the real birth into adulthood, away from the diseased malignant void of voracious hedonistic appetites. Into the valley of forgiveness and maturity. The righteous path that saves a sinner from becoming a troglodytic unappealing sociopathic rancid void of a being. Such a soul! What a hero!

Martin: What a martyr. I promise to be chaste forever, for the rest of my life, here and now to give up on all physical sin with another person. I'm only human, I can't be a saint, I mean it's impossible to keep absolutely clean isn't it? So then my all-encompassing Lord, to save myself from Hell, I promise absolutely to keep my celibacy for the rest of my life. Amen! May Arthur be proud of me.

John: Congratulations! You are free! Now all that's left before you is three years of penitence for every year of pleasure, that's about thirty years of penance, temptation and suffering and the worlds your oyster! Simple, concise, easy to apprehend the philosophy of truth is it not? VERITAS magnifico! If you survive those first initial seven years of trial and error, passing all obstacles and temptations, all will be well. Good luck with that by the way.

Martin: Indeed, there's hope for desperate souls lost to shameful weakness of the knees and joints rather twisting than straight. Woeful wayward journeys. A bent and crooked longing for some quick relief from shame does nothing but charge more of the same. Often, I see these lost and weary men park themselves to the spot and scream up at God, I will not go down! I will not be beaten! The Devil will not beat me! More power to their sails.

John: Tis the bodies and spirits of inconclusive monstrosities that he uses as his pawns, beware the mouths of fools, beware the thoughts of empathy headed idiots, enemies and rivals. Here in this time, here in this indigo covered valley where well waters cease and threats of eternal drought rule over the hand of men, lessons will be learned. Blindness no longer seeks to pave a way through the thickening thorn bushes. It's the quick and the dead. The heavy as lead, the wavering quaking earth built on sand that's sinking into the ever-deepening mire of perdition.

Martin: Yesits the quick and the dead indeed brother. Rivers of blood teach humanity nothing but its thirst for more suffering. Headless royals make great entertainment for jokers yet headless themselves after the circus closes for rivers of blood.. Oceans of blood no prophet can divide, no God can sustain against. No God is powerful enough, none but man can shed the tide and man forever bound by blood, dies with it.

John: Marvellous it is to know that Gods are limited, indeed its their very nature to be, for without opposition there would be no need for them. No contest, no limitations, no risks, all rewards, no line in the sand, no scripture on the walls, no demons, no devils, no pain, no suffering, no blame or catastrophe.

Martin: No famine, no plague, no ignorance nor shame, no hunger for dreams, no cold north winter winds. Just angels and dreams, wondrous streams, beginnings no endings, gold's eternal spending, marching miraculous, fantastic enigmatic perfections. Cosmic solutions, communal revolutions, more than before, an eternal cornucopia of giving gods and joy for everyone.

John: Sounds like a Summer festival in the mind of a thirteen year old girl. Utopian dreams in the pure suburban fantasies of the illogical supremely dreaming lover of unicorns, fairies and happy flower lands of Paradise. Ah, (Turns to audience, wouldn't that be lovely) Ah the minds of babes, the clean hands of a well bred child. Yes, as close to God as we can achieve, indeed it is. Right?

Martin: Rushed, hurried, anxiety ridden, panicked, bowled over in a sweaty cumbersome tarred and feathered frenzy. Afraid and fearful of misadventure, hearts beating with a healthy sporadic drum beat that sends the soul soaring in a raggletaggled bee line for the sanctuary of the gin bottle and the meat platter of the nest.

John: Energised only by compulsive disorders, unflattering furthermore disaster zones. Nervous system's shot to shell, badgered workforce near the edge, over indulged passions pledges forced reason out, battered senseless, frozen with doubt. Eternal retirement for the masses.

Martin: Meticulous sensations shuddering bones, unreasonable requests decantered, unknown orders lost in translation, follies floundering fluid membranes launched onto the floors of capital gain and infrastructures dysfunctional demise. Ah, yes, tis the end of days alright.

John: Yet humanities resilience abounds, clowns go down forever more, where greatness ceases not. Cold heartedness in fools, gives treason a reason, expels corruptions demise, ousts saviours remedies, accuses only the innocent.

Martin: Blinded confusions antidote, mourns the loss of pleasure, crawls' about in darkness with goblins of the ethers, ectoplasm and fortunes sold for golden souled cherubs and angels. Vengeance cries out in its impotence for to be saved finding only justice is the only revenge.

John: Baptised in fire the solitary warrior returns, bruised by demons and worn down allies, usually mindful of their hatred. Love lost for ancestral crimes, hideous violations of the youth in their prime. Souls reduced to diseased addicts, seeking solace in addictions of the body, soul and mind.

Martin: Wailing mourning spirits bound to a thousand years of eternal-like damnation stand upon the head of the lion as its roar trickles to a whimper. When all lions must bow before the Gods, for of the gods they're born. The energies of a hundred thousand reflect nothing on the spectre of a hundred million lives lost to well bred inbred royalties needs.

John: All nations equal in sin, go down for the final count, the bells toll, the rivers of Hell, the lands beneath hold no grudge on mankind. They know well that humanity suffers from Devils, from diseased dragons of dark matter, of the great God of opposition.

Martin: All cultures colonised, all have enslaved their futures, bound themselves to failure by greed, by creed, by acts of brutality, by rape, by thieving, by murder. All humans are guilty of sedation, hypocrisy, lies, treachery, apostasy, blame and terrorism. Adding their opinions to the minions.

John: Impulse to lose, impulse to choose, never solutions, conclusions reversed, crimes reimbursed, slipping like eels down water-worn boulders, cascading routes down waterfalls, down, down, down. For some its so easy to hold to their promise and keep to their pathways without failing or wailing, that's why their solutions conclude with more silver and gold. Instant cure for all the Divils ails.

Martin: Not many like that I'm afraid, yet for those who are blessed its necessary to be strong when all around them assume the position of the whore of Babylon. Men and women of course, must let go when the Moons at its height and all demons take flight high on their passages. Great offering have been made for humanities plight, so naive are their memories, so blind and obtuse. There's a tower watching from all four directions.

John: All four winds. High are the eagles on the wing, singing of ancient Gods, songs raised high where only angels hear the flight of Falcons song. The harps of Hibernia sing true for great is the heart of the Muse. Wonders never cease when love and honour rule.

Martin: Wise men sing praises with wise women, struggles for balance and harmony gather little without war of oppression. Governments fall, new countries are born, all rings true for prophesies calling. Bridge builders see failings and faltering in mankind. Still the good are fast and steady the course. Star bright high and mighty, all mapped out in Heavens dualities.

John: Mothers gain strength indomitable, unfettered fearless and brave, women roar like lions, children the same. New world orders of the spirit challenge those of finance. Truth speakers are heard only by their audience. For there are other speakers, spirit speakers whose tongues lie only for those that hear them.

Martin: Voracious manifestations of inclusive population. Magnificent manifestations, tidal waves of appreciation, omnipotent soaring spirits of great dominion and power rule over the word of saints and their flock. Tireless believers in faith hope and charity.

John: Sadly the baleful whores of Satan's kingdom slither from the gutters and abuse the children of the lord in all their innocence. The pigs of the pit, the imp infested demonically possessed scum of the universe. All full to the brim with the squalor and sloth of cheap alcohol and blame. Jezebels chosen people.

Martin: The hounds of Hell the Cerberus, cradle snatching vermin that stalk the weak and the lame, seeking justice for a scorned life. Roaring waves of unwelcomed advances on the youth with ugly eyes hidden behind the veil of horror and spiritual decrepit rancid hideousness. Here be monsters burying their prey out in the moors. Screaming to all the heavens how great they are.

John: Sewers fuel their bath houses, the sons of the rich lie down by the masters of the impoverished prostitute, all are equal in measure and disrespect. Humanity rotten to the core despises the good innocent children of the middle ground. Students of sin pull down the students of civilised education. One by one, by default, the vermin must gain ground. After all somebody has to go down.

Martin: Someone's soul must be equalised, put in their place, yet who deserves it? They think they're better than the child whose drunken fathers hate and despise them. They're victims of ignorance and pride, they must do what is willed of them. Overcome all obstacles and retrieve vengeance of the weak more sensitive youth whilst they still can. Direct truth sadly is often ugly.

John: Yes, the last sanctuary of sanity lies in the avoidance of the ordinary damned. The truly repulsive and rancid collective personality of imbeciles and the governments they support. The backward lay waters of an restricted mentality let loose on the infrastructure once ruled by Earth Religions, Druids and their flock, the Celtic warriors , Now thrown to the side of complacency and humiliation.

Martin: Yes, instilled pride beckons the bruising primate within, crashing down upon the head of the lion. Their terrorism reflects the evil hand not the royal civilised beast that prides itself in satin clothes and doctored laudanum, opiated bliss.

John: Vampires sucking on the lives of the innocent. Wars of the dark ages that cost more than any countries worth. Bankrupt for fear of invasions that never happened. Crumbling castles in the sand, what clowns Satin makes of vain superiority when imbeciles abound and drunken jesters manifest within bones of swine and hound.

Martin: Very poetic brother, indeed your tongue serves well to discern the truth of the eternally infested soul. Hell its a new millennium and why not celebrate the taste of furious Gods whose hands and eyes are trained on this motionless mob of headless corpses, empty vessels, moronic ever squabbling rabble. Squabbling greedy fearful faces consumed by all that opposes health and true riches untold. (Page 11)

John: Vengeance pours forth on humanities back like a tempestuous royal, spreading its empire on the earth worshipping Christians like an angered Pagan God. The Paganity of greed, of hedonistic blood thirst, the gods of destruction are no Christian Gods. They are the Gods of war, of death, the ravens of death. The breakers of bone and the burners of house and precious home.

Martin: Tis the time of judgement, the time of the evil eye, the confused pineal gland, the time of foreign hoards massing on the already stretched gold reserves of constitution. There's a plague beset on the homes of the old houses. Angry at their conversion to Christianity. The two thousand years has passed, the tests are eternal. The strength of mothers tests. The rewards for holding ground through great are short lived.

John: Vanity and pride hold the masses short of emotional fears as the tempest rises with the weather. Pig Headed women roar their infesting way through the lives of their more sensitive counterparts. Jezebels straight from hell roar and scream for more as they lose their souls in blame. Marauding Viking succubus seeking to destroy and conquer, to blame all men. Then turn on themselves when failure results.

Martin: Projection of that same fear, the fear of sin, the love of joy, the need for love, the hatred of fools. For whosoever the fool that destroys love, the man or the woman. The spiteful furies bent on revenge, the bitter twisted mind of the possessed soul. The child of the mother that demands only suffering from life. The all whoring Babylonian vermin of the earth crying victim! Victim!

John: Oh you're in trouble now brother. Malevolent dust storms are building their way towards you as we speak. Hoards of revenge fuelled daughters ride the backs of Valkyries to your door. Wreaking havoc for their unwelcomed passengers who are flung to the spirit as offerings to the new Gods. Sacrifices for hypocrisy, all to blame are the benevolent, all responsibility on mankind's unseen pillars.

Martin: For the armies, the rivers of blood spawn from the tombed out stomachs of modernity's rabble. Woeful tides of demons roar above the sound of those lost souls, those spirit children. Little hands never to see the light of day, for modern life is expensive, costs of living increase, fathers and gifts rejected never born give nothing but their drunken impotency to the world. Damned fools ever bent on truth or goodness.

John: I, who would blame those daughters of the mother, who would care for that child abandoned to chaos. Cries for help never heard, deafened ears directed away from such thoughts. Tis better to have a good weekend than slay that life again and again. Over the years as the wrinkles show, how vanity rules the heart of the slighted.

Martin: Each weeks end is a tide for life, the taste for more, the joy of spirit and injected opiate. Given the end of each week ads to the loss of hundreds of thousands of unseen lives. All those souls floating through the atmosphere, the spirits or unrecognised dreams. By week, after week, after week of Pans simple pleasures. Does lead to the ritualistic ectoplasms of blame and effect.

John: A hundred thousands unborn souls every single week the world around, now spirit children following their mothers, following their fathers who may not even know that spirits name. Shameful humanity knows little of remorse, yet many ay the same, many hold deer the souls that have been sacrificed to the Gods of modernity.

Martin: Yes, a blood sacrifice on the alters of Jezebel and Lilith's aides. Although to lose a life for reasonable reasons, a life is still a life. A soul may come back and try again with no major scars from its demise, plucked early from the womb in past life, returns again when the mothers ready.

John: True, though the Gods of destruction keep vigil on mothers rejections, the light of the divine allows for another day for life to bloom. Its catch twenty two as who blames who, when blamelessness should always be the key to diplomatic immunity.

Martin: So forgive us young mothers if we appear to be blunt, so true is life and it never asks permission nor does it seek fogginess when it comes crashing down at the inopportune times. What monsters' do we appear that know the absolute, yet patience we have none for humanity and its foibles.

John: Gentle overtures accounted for advancing orchestras of angels fly high o`er mountain tops to carry the light bearing souls their destinies. Golden moments of love and sparkling eyes full of love and free for a good upbringing compared to the dreaded Hell of impoverished unprepared and ready for more inebriated mistakes and only drunken heated dogs to blame.

Martin: I forgive your debt to societies suffering souls, your comment leaves little to the imagination. The horrors of existence do truly lie on our skins like bulging scars holding to memories for projections on our enemies. This testing time has many highs and lows, many fools that don't deserve to work have jobs when many skilled and mature people have not, or no longer can they suffer the injected demonic swine in the workplace.

John: True natures of man expect service from emancipated governments, all in al the corridors of power serve only to build debt and worship at the foot of lies and hypocrisy. All men must endure the poverty that lies in vainglorious self importance. Yet the people rule with honour on the paths laid out for them.

Martin: Good people rule as one against the ever increasingly sinister forces of the lost souls morbid paths. Swine souls of hedonistic pleasures at first glimpse seem oblivious to the destruction of the apocalypse and its subtle hidden ways.

John: The veil being lifted gains sway in the minds of the wise, of parents who reject their past activities and move on to higher ground. The four treasure of Ireland lye on their alters or upon the alters of heir priests. Groomed not are their children by the misguided parades. For al routes to paradise lie hidden within the soul body.

Martin: Elemental forces scriptured within the nervous system, within the body itself, a sensitive balance experienced close to the bones of hip and sockets al together. Wholesome normalities rule characterisation and the cauldrons within correspond to reasonable doubt.

John: Deep within the sphere of consciousness lies realities conversion, coherent to concepts regular exceptions to the norm. Exhibitionism and voices resourced overwhelm the bodies addiction to inevitable experimentations forced on the ore sensitive being unaware of the consequences to mind, body and soul.

Martin: Wild wind blow when trouble comes calling, biding its time for years of togetherness spent rambling the moors and bogs. Spirits of spiralling storms in the teacups of time wile away the bones of panicked pauper mentalities.

John: Woe is the mind that's blinded, woe are the arms of a fool, twisted and weak, woe be tide the roar of his enemies all banished form Paradise, all wailing, all bating their time for the broken rejected fool to return to his God once more begging to be saved.

Martin: Aye, tis true indeed the spread of pride, the rage of the slave in tow, of a thousand years of evil conquests. Its inverting primal reductions of normal human consciousness. Reverting back to animalistic impulsive instinctual unintelligent thought processes born from evil blood-thirsty scrapping pillaging modern armies of empirical dominions.

John: Destined for destructions inevitable surrender to the will of the beast. Clandestine monstrosities liberation within the sphere of secrecies hidden concealers prophesised expulsion of the spirit of mankind. Transmuted infections of the mouth manifest into incurable sexual disease, or more fashionable than post humously expected.

Martin: Sympathetic cultural discrepancies isolated expressionisms of denial. Artistic tendencies fight for celebrity status overwhelms the paparazzi in its race for extravagance, death and dysfunctional moral hygiene.

John: Obstruction of justice, the wild majestic dream of silence reveals boundaries burden salvations. Forging restless mountains furtive futures great achievements coveted creations. Omnipotent fantasies persistent solutions overwhelm recurrent dreams of denial and absolution.

Martin: Overburdened benevolent deities shed the waters of times failures, given they've had plenty of opportunities to see the light and then reject it. Representatives of both parties struggle for attainment, achievement and victory over each others eternal agendas.

John: Absolutely truthful realities are known to the good, the loyal to God and those whose tempers are vented in smashing objects and not other people. Humanities rejected souls are the chosen people, this world is equal and opposite, agree and disagree. Grey and grey make grey days and dull lives duller.

Martin: Developments reversed theoretical achievements dissolved by nihilistic monstrosities. Particular manifestations post-humorous fixations criminalities formidable creations partake in subtle stupidities vengeance on all sensitive souls.

John: Duplicities justice delivers equal blows on challenged intellects, retarded mental cognitions viral dysfunction. Creations of idiot mentalities absolute plague on normal sensitive people who are no longer allowed to function in rampant raging swine possessed hoards swinging their way downwards.

Martin: Spiralling vortex overwhelms all during the changing of seasons and monumental achievements abound. Constant winding of whirlwinds orchestration devising plummeting winds whirling subterfuge forces strong and compulsive. Eternal struggles rearing their ugly heads like bullying children starving in the playgrounds of government and court.

John: Magnificent challenges make for enormous sacrifices, serious characters without brains make gigantic asses of their memories. Control and domination over local rivals makes for neurotic obsessive compulsion and nothing much else. Alcohols usually to blame in these cases. Inherited abuse cases, possession on a grand scale.

Martin: Snivelling little personalities with nothing but their mouths as weapons set to kill on any potential rivals. Great is their battle, great their name, self delivered, don't need God, are God themselves in ego and id, of mind and bowel, small Gods, little ones, Lilith, Jezebel and their father, the beast.

John: Realities pessimistic reversal philosophies' manifested natural selections inbreeding monstrosities experienced in experimental in honourable reproduction of extinction. Programmed inconsistencies passionate journeys through frequent flyers obsessions with filth filled palsies.

Martin: Incorrigible virtues blessed by infected juries' condemnations manufactured sensory perpetrations of innocent victims biological freedom. Abolished morality welcomes death and destruction from destitute sociological realities friends of fortune fixated on escape, pleading for peace deals with vampiric colonial pride.

John: Fortunes fantastical excursions linear perspectives non-existent realities foreseen positioning occupied by silent empty vessels. Royal appendage dimensions patronising superiority compulsions fooling only themselves and not the reformed paupers one presided as second class citizens.

Martin: Terrible fate delivered to haunted structures of financial gain and fortitude, forced to build expensive ghettos in rejected areas concreted soulless grey wet winter voids of existence. Crucified spirits drawn ever closer to the bone of servitude to crowns, now in enormous debt themselves.

John: Tragic separatists' rebel against denials ever promising extinction of nihilistic fairy tales failure to produce. Ever dyslexic border crossings multitude of morbidly boring procedures duplicate ancient communistic tragedies. Intuitive divulgence of bubonic political satire and operatic catastrophe.

Martin Hieroglyphic symbolism reveals our existential reverberation of sedated Vesalius theories manifesting in ever decreasing intelligent human minds. Measured monstrosities hypothermic nucleus superiority complex appears inferior to epic-dominant sub-cultural contra lateral Neanderthals.

John: Ventral digestions ventriloquistic relationships blinded by the dorsal diagrammatic need to destroy any non-quadrille beasts. That's human beings indeed where metaphysical monstrosities manifest in millennium bacterial medial three dimensional specifications.

Martin: Indeed (looks at audience with eyes wide) Lateral undefeated sidewinders access formidable anterior political posteriors subterfuge. Habitual rostral invasions caudal meticulous functions reverberate naturally within the standard corridors of power. Whew!

John: Absolutely! Coronas crowned royal forces intricate rectal transverse sections overwhelm the opposition and rule supreme for quadruple embarrassments for all. Sagitale sections wavering corruptions parasitical horizons focussed more on financial gain rather than the poor misguided people.

Martin:Surgical instructions subdivisions neuroanatomical representation of government muses labelled developments. Aneurisms dissected with normal cosmetic instruments way beyond the comprehension of the voting publics id. Never ending eternal dysfunction better of hired than fired government bodies.

John: Central cortex creates Olympic sized symptoms within the hidden and concealed. Teutonic superior structures reveal only inferior policies retarded techniques and miniscule abilities to rule supreme. Structures subdivisions develop appetites for survival rather than success in a world gone mad for financial gain, there lies only financial shame.

Martin: The Gods ignored now blamed for humanities self-inflicted cancerous self-delusionary rules. It's all the Devils little helpers anti-divine path to the void. The Gods are busting their guts keeping the evil down as it is, they can't answer every selfish little prayer from the little people.

John: Isolateral and elemental contrasts contralateral political spiritual choices, its so simple! (Looks at audience) Optical construction of dilapidated potters' tool Masonic industrial cities, slowly developing in spits and spats as economies desperately try to survive the financial apocalypse they're all so desperate to deny.There's joy in repetition.

Martin: There's joy in repetition. That's human selective physiology at its best, zero visual perception unless basic human survival on rising costs can be avoided. Sheep by action sheep by nature, blind sight theories intact techniques free the fugitives of the last millennium. History repeats itself. All gibberish algebra.

John: Right! Sacrificing intelligence is the path of the intelligent. A wealth of kisses endless infinite paths to paradise lye in the hands of children, open in mind and free from ignorance until they inevitably encounter it via their educational system. Ironic isn't it? (Looks at audience)

Martin: Hawk headed heroes and heroines at play in the fields of the Lord, running fearlessly the straight paths to illusions and dreams. Where realities truth reveals a world of awe and fantasy, joy and adventure. Whose hand is it that blinds the youth to life's true joys. What disease takes away the heart of a young aspiring artist to dash it by the rocks of failure and desperation.

John: Well ask any successful artist and they will tell you there's a wealth of wisdom in the world, but sadly all art is popular art, unless its religious. Yet spirituality allows for elasticity between the subject and its muse. When a child draws a tree its more than a tree, it's an enigma, for the child and those lucky enough to have been chosen to see it.

Martin: Were not monsters after all, (Turns to audience) Who would smite a dictator and their soldiers if he had those God-like powers to turn the tide of colonial invasion? Well, that's the world we live in today is it not? Who would reach out and defend smaller nations from tyranny? Well only those with enough reason and power. The reason being fear or money.

John: No Gods there then, just playing God. There is a difference is there not? The oafish orangutans overture blasting away at the mountains of the earths golden majestic display. Diamonds for everyone, never-ending need to reap the Goddess, solid storage where the mountains move from the earths caverns to manmade ones beneath sweetly cobbled stone Swiss streets.

Martin: Gold teeth as far as the eye can see, a beautiful country though, but a small planet, mores the pity. Metaphorically speaking of course, tis an enormous rock we inhabitate is it not? Mores the point of rescue, general psychiatric assessment of the collective disorder that encompasses the schizoid situation that's presented before us here today. (Looks at audience raising his eyebrows, nodding)

John: Virtuous patience gradual approval for special situations nothingness rules supreme over severed emotional bondage. Transformed universal degradations controlled mental connection. All maximum points manifest in tried and tested techniques impoverished insanity forcibly denied.

Martin: Separatists now accepted as normal millennium revolutionaries with reasonable peaceful protests, abound, screaming for change, then having more of the same. Stressful situations lead to venting of political views as important, without having an aneurism or resulting in death, chest pain or vascular discomfort.

John: Dissection indeed is the cure where prevention is unavoidable though fascist reactions from leadership isn't necessarily a mature response any day of the week. Populations push and shove creating controversial results calling into question their diplomatic abilities. Circumstances aside. The rolling mob, bone crushing density of ignorance.

Martin: Intrepid voyages usually lead to colonisation of the free tribes of the earth. True discovery lies in their resurrection and recovery. Altruistic abominations oxymoronic achievements force the stubborn to flee towards their true destinies.

John: Where true destinies lye, where wanderers roam where angels rest, where solitude returns, where the solitary to the womb return. When solace moves fate to fortune, when hope reveals reward, when vice turns to virtue, when Christ rules over Rome.

Martin: How heavens rule dominates confusion, where innocents reveal the truth, how well mothers love their little children, where purity is revealed before the veil. Well is the hand that is clean and consecrated, blessed and washed of all ills and wrong deeds.

John: Strong are the hearts of righteous people, disciples of the light, overcoming evil in all its ancient masks and guises. Scarred warriors hardened by their lives can whip young inexperienced idiots raring for their vice.

Martin: The world is changing, now we are the gate keepers, the watchtowers for our children, mothers become priests, fathers bless and purify. Silence virtues rule supreme, blessings of light rule where giants used to roam and crash and bound through the lives of their flock.

John: Access all areas, all gains and restraints rejected in alchemical unions and bonds. All light of divine intervention reveals solutions resolved. Burdens offloaded, strength returns fires banished and more confidence if God returns.

Martin When mental arithmetic exposes truths before concealed, lights flashing realities expand the consciousness of angels and our true nature. Evangelical responses confided in secrets for the chosen few. Yet they shine themselves as individuals of society, its structures and all developments of humanity.

John: Repetitive mistakes undone find solace in human frailty, all humans have enemies, yet all are each other's. The enemy of the self lies within, deep inside the shadows of doubt linger. No human lives a perfect life, yet many strive for perfection, harmony and love. Those that do gain it greatly within.

Martin: Sophistication in society leads to democratic oaths and in itself to destruction by powerful egos defending their right to self-depreciation. God is gold and gold should be worshipped in the idols of God, then stolen by marauding colonising foreign invaders, by default, to show humanity their weaknesses, thus making them stronger. Strange the melting of Pagan Mayan Gods are reborn to become Golden crucifixes for the alters of Rome.

John: Me thinks you jest. The kindling of the flame within should be extinguished by foreign marauding colonists bent on the reduction of intelligent life. Maximization of suffering equals the enormous profits made by colonisation usually by the ancient race that colonised it in the first place. Plus, the bloodied golden Mayan idols are far from Christ's blood by the twinkle of a fraction.

Martin: Thus, modern colonial religions expanding their territories and ancient philosophies on unsuspecting foreign peoples, using their own gold against them. Decimation of values, bloodlines, languages, religions, doctrine, self-respect, equality, all marched through the furnace of foreign invaders enslaving local hero's and their children. Recycled Paganism becomes the God of the Sun, the light, water into wine, then blood. It must have confused the local tribe's people somewhat.

John: Yes, very profitable for the rich getting richer and their warriors building a bridge to fame and prowess. To be out shined by fools and imbeciles is the fate of the fallen, there is no greater suffering than the suffering of spiritual failure. Perhaps some gold should stay in the earth where it belongs. Priests drinking the blood of Christ before a congregation of Pagans, must have reminded them of their own outlawed spiritual beliefs.

Martin: What confusion reigns before the masses, truly thought is the enemy of servitude. No greater stress than anger towards the self, no weakness than that of the body that fails the warrior in times of testing. Greater patience greatly needed for accuracy and acute, adept and skilful adaption to surrounding adherence of millennium madness. Humanities blood keeps the gold flowing, does it not?

John: Adoration of anachronized belief system's deteriorate rapidly in adulation of weaknesses and addictions to self-absorption. Aesthetics of self-improvement affable aloof agrarian policies repulsive altruistic generosities. Amending local constitutions adverse reactionary side-effects of idiotic thought processes. And yes, it does indeed.

Martin: Regardless as to the frailties of humanity, vigilance pays, health stays the course, readies the blood for action, gives motions devoted to the norm. Extraordinary misadventures inexplicable extension before the heated circulations corpuscles rise beyond measures flustering devotion to the course and fictitious lies wordsmiths invention.

John: By golly that's a tongue twister of alternate dimensions intravenous degrees involved for reasonable doubts in tested citations. Ramped unification soothes to triviality the leisure's of paramount elation. Monumental magnificent conversions revile poor-mouthed optional vacations, occupied in casual causes far beyond the norm.

Martin: Monumental changes only the gifted can see as clearly as their own misguided weaknesses.

Act Two

John: (Enters stage right, dressed in a white cloak, green tunic or shirt, red shoes and black sash, holding a staff with a lantern on the top, a stable solid lantern, not the kind that hangs down.)

John: Ode to the soul that has come prepared, has followed the roads golden mile, steadied the pace, rolled with the winds of change, listened through his ears and seen through his own eyes. Ah yes the practical mind and its joyous gifts indeed do bother. Here is my brother, Martin. (Points to backstage at the entrance, stage centre, a black door with a white handle.)

Martin: (Enters wearing a long black cloak, wearing a white tunic, red shoes and a green sash across his chest, holding also a staff with a solidly attached lantern or lamp atop of it)

Martin: You look smart old friend, here to the joy indeed of all souls lost yet returned unto me sayeth the lord of light. The destroyer of worlds, the victor in war, defending the homeland, to whom go the spoils.

John: Great are the wavering masses that decree, their youth are forever bound to suffer the whipping place of this great world. Take the lash, pay the piper, stay the course and devour all that block your way.

Martin: Fallen are the rich into decay, so it will be as its been written.

John: For ten thousand years how popular indeed has modernity delivered in times of specialist destruction and doom. Quiet offensive to divine order, higher beings, their angels and their un-

38

flawed philosophies on evolution.

Martin: Final triumphs industrial realties devotional conversations, accepted agreements of normal situations. Bound to fruition, strapped to realities invented new motions for the brain. Gracious intelligent, sensitive human beings living on an continents of ignorant dishevelled imbacilles, themselves obsessed about their appearance.

John:Halleluiah, the truth at last, our journey through other strangers' lands. The exodus of immoral joyful jesters, beset upon their masters, the eternal takeover, theirs from beggars to kings, from clowns to world leaders, all for the buck, all for the taste of some other man's wife, some lost civilisations blatant scourge. What a world this is.

John: There are some that see only what the good lord shows them, forjust a glimpse of truth the down the pillars groundlings base, they lie in wait for dirty sinners haste. Frog and toad, unholy hoards forgive the ways of humanity.

Martin: Watchers folly blames another, hidden truths are soon discovered. Neath the covers of the veil, lies deceit where truth prevailed.

John: Bent and broken spines of sinners, youth discarded in the piles of blame. Suffering souls with cancerous skin, smoking mountains wait within.

Martin: Then the cry of new-born saint, awaits his fate, forgets his destiny. Here be monster's large as mountains, building bridges straight and narrow, some above the call of duty, studious servants of illusive cruelty.

John: One man'sact, another's folly, unaccountable games lay waste, for the devil's favourite tastes.

Martin: Oh, how wonderful it is, letting memories at ease, forget the past and break new ground, just remember those simple truths, never sleep, never lye silent, never forget, never gives up, the wounded heart of the human sinner.

John: Weakness comes in many guises, pushed upon the weak surprised. One day here the other gone, its fate that rules our human home.Bones break, miracles mend, monies spent, debts paid, reapers rated, surplus spirits abated.

Martin: Wholesome follies market well the eyes favourites, beauty stills the heart, pleasures painful perdition blends into waters deep. Mistakes made repeated until habits form from daily use. More than enough experience makes a master of pleasures pain. Penitence pleasures, burdens leisure's.

(Woman enters, wearing a High Priestess style dress, with goth like make up, not over the top, just subtle enough to be seen. She moves her hands gracefully by her sides in a ballet type movement of sensual, seductress, sorceress from time to time to connect to the audience with her energy.)

Womans name is Lilith.

Lilith: Hitherto I see, this new world belongs to me, more so then the Lord you call the father of all, from one ocean to another. Mighty all powerful Jehovah, does suffer greatly his chosen peoples smitefull suffering, does he not?

John: Speak your words spirit, for all to hear, there's no message you have for us two, by the powers that be, you will know this. Born and raised by it you are and will be again. Speak if you must.

Martin: Be still when the word is upon you and we will stay the power for now, speak your piece,

Lilith: Little do the people know of Gods and Kings, more so of the serpent's tale does slip through tongue's and end in Hell.

Small the mind of weak and blind, lame the hand that smites all men.

Hand in hand with spirits dark, their tongues a grey and filthy strain.

Stand outside their doors awaiting, set aside for suffering and hatred of the same.

John: What wonderfully descriptive rhetoric.

Martin: We are charmed indeed to have such delightful company.

Lilith: This be the time of judgement, yet from a source unknown to sinful and wicked.

Damnation swarms about the living, building bridges of anxiety and fear.

Darkening skies, wild weathered untethered rain and wind.

Calling out for a God that no longer seems to care.

John: Well lets not despair shall we?

Martin: Hope springs eternal does it not, cheer up it not all that bad is it?

Lilith: More to the time there are the good, Ill give you that, they hide from the world in the safety and warmth of their homes. I have babies too, they are loved and nurtured by my side. Yet mankind seeks to injure his with selfishness and pride.

John: Such is life.

Martin: No one is free of guilt.

Lilith: Much of more, that we adore the beautiful endorphins, deep within that bloodied corpse, that hanging minstrel, that woeful dictator beneath. There's a fellow worn to death by suffering, bone to the edge, beaten and whipped by his own.

John: Cheerful.

Martin: Uplifting.

Lilith: Sold my soul for my fathers hand had taken more than his fair share from left and right, from up and down, from foreign lands. Endless slaves, jewels priceless, Nubian flesh, endless gold and silver mines. Ruled the known world and called it his own, for as far as the eye could see.

John: She speaks of the Carpenter and of The great King, the father of David.

Martin: True indeed his power was eternal, even for a mortal, his spirit lives on in his people.

Lilith: Truth in bounty sayeth the book, riches untold promised for all that strive for truth. There lies truth in lies, justice in sin, freedom in all the seven deadly sins. Freedom from hypocrisy, for that is all we see in the hands of holy men, their gold, their lands, their riches untold, as far as the eye can see. All that they see before them is there's for the taking, is it not?

John: Blessed art thou..(Lilith holds her hands up to him in anger.)

Lilith: Stop! Imbecile! Thy God lies not in my chamber.

Martin: Our Father who art in heaven...(She holds her hands up to him also and seethes through her mouth.)

Lilith: Enough damned fool! Hold your tongue, I will not stand for these words, you must let me say my piece, then I will begone. There's a truth in lies and a liar finds peace in consuming such things.

John: Speak your piece.

Martin: Speak, then be gone, there are devils awaiting your soul in that lair you call your abode.

Lilith: Fair indeed it is that place I reside, there within the bodies where ancient sinners lie. Neath the flour, down under, resting, awaiting for fallen enemies to devour. Suckling on the souls of the innocent, prey and fodder for every family has one. The chosen servants of death and evil. The last bastion of a stolen mind.

Discontinued efforts in goodness, wherever it tried, tried, tried the failed, for no-one expected less. The scapegoats rest is deep within the potter's ground there's lies the sinner.

John: Still she does share our own message, perhaps there is purpose in her story after all, continue.

Martin: As above so below, still beneath and beyond the veil.

Lilith: Seeking beauty in all things, so messiahs sing of Summer breezes. Pleasure for pleasures sake, stills the soul's journey when too much is never enough. When too little substance and quality begins to vanish from the hands of non-believing vanquished hedonistic sinners.

Then my sisters take their weight in soul, swathed in the lifelessness of mankind's failing store. Mores the pity there will always be war and pestilence, death and starvation. Vendetta against the innocent, yet on they plunder, deeper and deeper into my master's territory.

John: Half and half, there are two kingdoms lest we forget, one that shares where the other sells its wares.

Martin: The holy mother (Lilith makes a face and holds up her hands in disgust) does rule the celestial heavens, also the Purgatorial underworld where many souls await their portals to higher ground.

John: Hope springs eternal for one side, waver thin for the other, so it is, so it shall always be.

Lilith: Though in my master's lands, all that waver fail to see, this light your carpenter brings the blind. Those that cannot see his light come to mine own and have their eyes returned, for all they see is black and evil futures there.

Those that cannot hear will then hear the sounds unheard by good souls, by the innocent, by the free. Their entire being will suffer greatly, their pain immeasurable, their screams heard for eternity, that is the music of evil, the beauty of absolute, the joy and rage my king gifts upon mine ears, my prise the sound of Christian tears. Joy to my soul's journey.

Hobbled Hell for legs once strong will falter there, for the hand of the damned, the fool, the sinful wicked non-believer, does stay his foot on rock and alter. That place brings justice, toil without mercy, great pains, injury, failing, suffering, insufferable weakness to the mind. Insult and injury to all God's children as they enter lives of hedonism found only in Sodom and the new cities now fallen.

A bashing of the brains, their name destroyed, their confidence shattered, their loins whipped by evil so terrible, so insufferable they beg and scream for it all to end. Without mercy they lie there as animals in filth, given respite only when my master calls them to bring his gifts back to the land of mortals. Earthquake is more than a metaphor and tidal waves pour over the living.

John: This be the spirits of our world, we suffer their whips all throughout our lives, my God have mercy.... (Lilith holds her ears in pain.)

Lilith: Stay your tongue Saint!

Martin: Know the power we hold over you spirit, stay your hand in this here place or we will speak our masters name and whip your head for its shame. Beware the power of our lord, for his might is great, his hand an awesome weapon, more than any demon in hell!

44

Lilith: True your master rules the light and over the Light bearer his name outshines our greatest warriors, our minions of impish demons and their favourite imbecilic human souls. The low vibrating spirits of ignorant swine, the troglodytes that smite your pillars, our little piglets as you have yours, so too do I.

John: My dreams last night had fair journey for myself, yet the gates of Hell where open wide, for trainloads of waxen sinful weakened souls piled up high did pass me by.

Martin: Truetwas the same dream had I, where I saw such woefulhorrific things, abominations of the bodies even in the living captors caught between this world and The Potters Ground. Like their molecules where swimming, their backside wide as the great oak tree, their heads shrunken too small to see, just abominations of eternal suffering.

Lilith: Well, for as long as this world lasts, as long as a moment in time, as swift as a candle is extinguished, is the memory of the damned, for a lifetime of hypocrisy is dually prophesised to be rewarded with suffering beyond human experience. An art of its own, as equal and opposite to your Paradise, as sure my master did almost rule it in his days of glory.

John: Well so too does man rule high, then does he fall, so to those awaiting failure rule upon the head of the lion and his offspring, such is the way of things. Royal for one millennium, pauper the next. Empires of blood and bone fall into the oceans andthe seas, eventually.

Martin: So true the will of evil, so good the justice and cause of suffering, for some fool's action takes the life of his own. For some evil fool's mouth causes the death of her own. Here there be many mouths that serve your master, many hands do his bidding. More so the office of the people that governs their fate, their servitude, their debt,their inheritance.

Lilith: Their enemies' souls. For in Hell, every Kings a beggar beset upon by his enemies, every Queen beheaded and her blood drawn by the quarter. There a mass of unhappy vile repugnant lowly slaves to the seven sins, for the seventh level of that suffering place. And well in league they are with their glorious master, the imp that inhabits them.

John: No rich men in Heaven, I always wondered why. So does it go, how boring indeed.

Martin: So true, for there's a servant in each quarter. This spirit amongst us does indeed serve her calling. There's work in this, for the human condition suffers greatly the spirits beneath, the mind cannot commit to the divine if its sickened by its body's addictions.

Lilith: You compliment reality sir.

John: Perhaps I do, you also reflect the work beyond goodness, the tides that wash away all grime and sewage. The heavy rains that clear about all traces of wrong doings, there must be those guardians of suffering and perdition.

Martin: The hounds of the underworld, they serve to enslave evil doers.

Lilith: They do, you are wise in your ways. My kingdom serves to keep your kingdom safe for the innocent ones. Their mothers be my sisters too, although they banish my sisters with their prayers and that condition known as servitude to superstition.

John: Our lord allows for such things, yet they be frowned upon by the masters of our church, it is allowed to bind those beasts of madness and sleep disorders with some thorny twigs wrapped in heather and wild garlic.

Martin: There's wisdom in the old ways, the power of herbs, the riches of root and bells, many in the mountains know well, the Pooka lives amongst the sheep and cattle.

Lilith: Yes, the spirits of the Sidh serve not God nor Devil, its well known to us to avoid these magicians of the Tuatha. Even the evil one himself avoids confrontation with the powerful Sidh, they serve nor God nor the Devil. Their magic is strong, their heads abound about the ethers, their countenance is of humanities confused state of mind, their true gifted arts are both holy and unholy.

John: Thus, they serve both The Devil and God by their very nature. For sure it's true both sides have their say in where humanity wanders and where they stay. Many the poor soul enters not Paradise nor The Potters Ground, bound to this earthly plane for an eternity, cold and forgotten, floating about the living as unwelcome as they may be welcome, like a bothersome child.

Martin: Cruel is the nature of this existence, heavy the toil and heavy the toll, war solves nothing nor peace leaves nothing in the wake of war. True that natures destroys man as man destroys nature.

Lilith: We are all bound to this existence one way or the other, both man and beast, there is no escape from toil, no comforts in modernity, just pollution for the mind, the body and the soul. For all that serve my master suffer in his wake. He holds no care for any humans, they all fall under his whip, they all suffer the stones thrown by their hateful, smiteful enemies.

John: Joyful pictures indeed, not for the innocent, nor the gentle, far from the charitable benevolent of spirit. Wise the works of other sides, soullessness rides thy blemished heart, the broken will, the steadied hand fears not life's whipping post. The everyman that rallies the darkness of death, fights the good fight and never gives up on God!

Martin: True the beast within man's heart strives to hobble his legs, take his wife and children down, breaks his will wherever it can and delivers nothing but enemies and fools to take all he has achieved for their own soulless needs.

Lilith:Gone are the trees that covered our ground, dry are the vast oceans of blue waters deep, high upon the greatest mountains lye countless hoards strewn about, where angels fear to roam.

John: Merciless is the lord, when angered by lecherous cowardice and sin.

Martin: Far from love and light, the hands of our saviour.

Lilith: True there are sounds bellowing from that void, where no being should ever have wandered. Darkness and weakened warriors fallen on their swords, bent to sinfulness and far from their master's reach.

John: Ever does the cry for hope strengthen the hearts of honourable and righteous men.

Martin: Greater patience upon the mind is needed for the grace of light in theses dark days.

Lilith: Sweet is the mind that's sees nothing in choice, leaves nothing to conscience, devours all and gives back still nothing. Great are the hands of the innocent when there's a chance of love taken from every heart they see. Straight from the belly of innocence lies a dormant demon in wait, spirits abounding on the dancefloor of adolescence.

John: Sweet is the night, romantic and bright, long are the days, wise in their ways.

Martin: Hours for the lovers, virginal youth, true believers in mystery, sleepless nights sought for dreams of love and glory.

Lilith: All dream of love, all break their hearts on fallen vows, the broken bough, the worn roots, the brittle tree-trunks fallen in tempestuous storms. Times immortal illusions pertain to overflow when rivers rise and bursting dykes account for metaphors morbid demise.

John: Tepid transformations diamond executions, burning martyr's paralysis over accountable recoveries. Deep is the heart that fights for what is right. Empty the heart that fights with a word, yet whose presence if far from the fray.

Martin: Sadly, all wars are fought by the everyman, the soldier stands with the slave. The saviours fall to disgrace as only empty vessels, seeking veneration for glorious fallen empires.

Lilith: There lies the rub, for whom the bell tolls that formulates perfection, thus mankind first kills the man, then fortunes are built on his inventions.

John: Stay the while for pities sake, a life less ordinary lies before thee, higher than mere sickless souls, more told than mitre, more fuelled than blood, higher than the greatest kings, are you not in your own kingdom.

Martin: Stay the while reveal their sights, grievous light here fly's the night of righteous men before the slayer. Ego verses vanity, blackened steel paves its way through earthly domains beyond the pale.

Lilith: Silver tongued are you both, mores the pity, my master's abode is fuelled by the souls of damned imbeciles. Hobbled Master of Human misery from western lands obsessed with winters death and cold disgrace, battling demented clowns, bitter endings for humanities leaden age, fraught infested astral domains, worried to death, their mothers' nerves at an end. Building bridges for no child's futures, deeper into debt as all royal roads lead, for a spell indeed, cheap as only fettered men will be.

John: There's an empty art in evil, a wasted word, a wasted stroke of painted brush on canvas, for our greatest are all weakened fools, all shallow vessels, damned rule breakers. Darkened doorways taken from the rejected, undiscovered geniuses' rule, where once where giants, now darkened dreadful pools of dread and doom.

Martin: Stay the course all hands in time, some child has gifts beyond the mind, there lies escape until the grudge, beyond endeavour, breathing blood.

Lilith: Well you know our ways, and still there's hope for evil to end up in paradise, before its time. Before judgment places its bornless hands over the veil, ousted all before them, into pale light as the setting sphere enters darkness.

John: What greater peril to destroy, our precious Heavens from the hoards. To see their ignoranceprevail in Celestial Kingdoms where no beast deserves to wander.

Martin: Still the fall from grace is here, for all to see, to touch and taste the rotten apples from the haunted gardens left to waste, the beast behind the veil. The silken worms do weave their webs.

Lilith: Great is the insult to your humanity, wondrous the filth that serves in Rome, hideous the horrors to the children of Eden, great the cancerous growth of Hell.

John: There's some taste for the poetic in your song, for all reversed is gone, all that's evil is sung, all that come will go, forgotten like the winds of change, for imbeciles no memories have. That is why they live so much closer to the Sun.

Martin: Great is the power of Christ! (Lilith holds her ears and screaming moans of pain come from the house speakers) There never will be an end to The Celestial rule of the angels, for night will have day, man and woman, good and evil, bright and dark, genius and Plebite!

Lilith: Stay that name. Your carpenter is an all-powerful punishment, of this we know, your bravery is rewarded, please sirs have mercy on my soul. I will away, No! (She stamps her foot at St John and turns to leave the stage as John threatens to sprinkle some holy water at her he has taken up from the edge of the stage floor. He sprinkles the doorway and the floor where Lilith stoodwith the holy water.

John: The power of Christ comes, this filthy soul back into Hell! In the name of the father, the son and the holy spirit Amen. (Places water back to stage edge out of sight.) God bless her twinkle toes, or not.

Act Three

A Man enters wearing rams' horns on his head, green twisted horns in a wizard style eyebrows and goatee beard, staff of magic by his side, powerful looking yet eyes glazed. His name is Warlock.

Warlock; May I enter here this sacred space, I will cause no harm, as above so below, so mote it be! (Holding his arms upwards and out in a cheerful stance, seeking welcome and invitation)

John: Enter Wizard, cause no harm, do unto others and no harm will come to thee also, you have my word.

Martin: Hitherto strange tales have come for your words are known above and below. Therein fixed upon that place and bound to it, as all fallen angels are.

Warlock: Fixed upon that place where angels be, barred from Hell, banished from the celestial plane. For what gods dwell upon the minds of men, where does evil go, where are the people when war passes by their doors? What Gods then rule the minds of men, slaughtered by each other's hands? Holding forth this staff of mine, I call upon the Pagan deities, rulers of the mountains, strength of thunder, might or wonder, slaves and plunder. No one knows more than me. Tis my domain your God watches over, sure he guides the weak and heals the lame, yes, he saves the innocent from evil, if their families are good and true. But he has now, cannot and will not hold back the waves of the great flood, nor can he stop the fiery molten rock from flowing oer the people's heads. Yet I can! (He blasts his staff off the stage floor to the sound of

thunder and lightning as the stage lights offer some display, unless a screen at the back of the stage can display a lightening flash
etc.)

John: (Amazed) Fantastic! My God! True powers do the wizards
hold, we deny this not. Understood. It's not an easy life, at best
there's a compromise in the world of spirit, fair weathered friends
fall apart, black and white pour into their own moulds a grey veil
of strife, waif-like that's hard to see.

Martin: Wondrous is the work of the spirit people, old is the
world, older than the New Gods are your children, this we see, we
are not blind to the truth of the old kingdom, for true there is evil
in war. Man takes vengeance on his enemies, this is true. It can be
a godless world for us all at times. Yet wizards have their ways, for
evil you are not, not as the Sun has its storms.

Warlock: There's no harm that's come to any child by the Goddess
great, the pure Nemain, the golden hearted Aine of the Moon. Forever and a day their bright light has shone down upon my race.
No laws we had to banish any priests nor law, no lies to sell, no
saviours outlawed or martyred. This we know is the way of modernity. See where it lies and ruins all that nature holds true.

John: Well its believed for ancient ruins tell, there's more in
heaven than in Hell.

Martin: Lands abound where spirits roam, banished from paradise and unwelcome in the underworld.

Warlock: Stay the course of time, many the soul that's entered
Paradise in one reincarnation, flows into the Potters Ground via
the next. Four score intensions mankind never cease to amaze,
then pitifully disgraces his good name in misadventure and the
seven deadly sins. From one God to the next, from health to ill-
health and back again. Fat as the lamb and rolling down through
insufferable insult, just to outlive his insulters as they leave this
life unloved and despised as the ignorant should well be.

John: There's a taste of victory for all sides, our aster and yours do collect their rewards, one soul up, the other down.

Martin: Well one saint finds his victories in vanity, for his people demand that same sin from their heroes.

Warlock: There's an insufferable pain in pleasure. For many men are failed by your master, there the rub. For what insanities lie bare in this here place today. For my master has ruled upon this tribe for eight thousandyears, long before your God arrived and stole their lands away. Where was he when their language was beaten out of them? Where was he when they had their lands strewn into almost uninhabitable islands of mud and stone. Where was your Damned benevolent and all powerfulGod then!

John: be still sir, you are frightening the locals.

Martin: The holy one. My master cannot intervene with the punishment of innocents, you know the reasons and the wherefores of these acts. For one fathers' sin, a sin delivered on the innocent, there is no hand of my master in death or punishment of the innocent, that is all The Evil Ones work and well you know it.

Warlock: Well I know and well I see your God does save innocent lives, picked them out before their death and just in the nick of time. Be The Evil One your enemy, not mine, my Gods have no fear of devils or their masters.

John: That be only good deeds done by man to save a life by the undoing of their sin.

Martin: Aye, well said good saint, when death comes for the innocent, perhaps one may walk away where none others can, for some good deed that's done to undo their family's demonic past.

Warlock: All families hold hidden facts from their own sweet souls. That is known to all the imps that drive within each soul, moving within likeplayful parasites through generations of damnation. One soul sinsupon a man, his hand is bound to his own. He takes a hand in war, one of his own loses an arm wherever his world may take it.

One young Empress is taken against her will, the hand of the sinner leaves a bloodline to his own untilthe debt is paid by seven to three. Each generation carries the weight, until a child is born, an innocent Empress whose path is clear and free for the joyful glories of all life's dreams and ambitions. Swiftly will she be taken by the beast and broken until the day she dies a wounded veteran of some drunken imbecilic relatives'sins, long passed into the potters ground before her.

John: Rest those souls, for all souls have sinned in past lives. All leave debt behind for spouses and children to bare on their backs. Hope springs eternal sir, the good prevails, the light follows the darkness.

Martin: Truth in justice, patience prevails, by the by, from angers wrathful vengeance overwills the will to murder ones spiteful idiotic enemies. The lowly man of the market stall, who's muscles grand, no brains at all, will conquer princes with his youth, willlive to see his offspring routed from their beds by the rich bankers slighted mind.

Warlock: true the beast lives amongst lowly men, the dogs of war, the drunken soldiers, blown to bone in wallowing waters. Endless hungers due to the royals and the rich.

John: The land of man is full of wonder, ceaseless roads to ease his slumber, yet sleep holds quick to sloth and greed, the hand of one lets the others bleed.

Martin: Deep the wounds and high the price, hard the penitence before enemies new. Few the more fearful swarms, ready to die for vain ignorance.

Warlock: You're ahead of me.

John: Paths intertwined my friend, your path leads this way eventually, tis only the Suns strong light that banished you into dark places.

Warlock: This my path has indeed lead into the darkness of great dragons, for in every old woman, who's rosary beads are flung into the service of herself and family. Their prayers are cast outwards so that all enemies must be smit `ed by their lord.

Deep within the bowels of ignorance lies the birthing seed for powerful men. Born of ignorance into a world of power and corruption. Here, where the good educated people see, their taxes spent eternally on evil things, where debt grows greater with every passing life and behind every bad man, there's a bad woman, believe me.

No entrance into hells punishing swell for these charitable beasts, who's faces shine on the worlds stage. They too prey, for more money and power, they kill to survive, they grease the palms of the important few. These heartless harmful swine, do stay here on this plain for all of eternities new born babes to fear, the smell of the fool, The footfall of the poltergeist, unwelcome in your Paradise, nor does the beast allow for Christians that prey into his realm, for tis only the truly damned that enter The Potters Ground.

John:Stay the course, your work is known to our master, it's the way of the ancients, the path to Perdition, for the ignorant must suffer. Thy must see the giants above them can do nothing where the soul is emptied by ignorance and blame.

Martin: True, there are many that worship at the door of blame, superstition their addiction, blasphemy their reward, yet banished are their children from the glories of life. There are great rewards for the living, indeed we too can se the faults behind Dogma, reduced to babbling fundamental faults. Hilarious the mouths of the hypocrite priests, they have a front row seat in The

Potters Ground, as well you will know.

Warlock: Fodder are some who's inheritance comes from the ignorant. Selling their culture as emptied vessels, singing songs of blame for invasions caused by their own hands. Rampaging villains from far away lands cannot be, without invasions from their own people first.

Blown to the four corners of this world, the drunken slaves, their cultures name sullied by their filthy ways. Horror comes in many guises, sullied are their names by enemies' tongues. Far the road and thin their hope, for criminals' greatest crimes are sold in conquerors place.

John: This be true, indeed there's mercy in banishment, no sensitivity in a nation of penniless paupers, drinking themselves to death from one continent to another. Devolution of that good name, barely hanging onto any semblance of self respect.

Martin: deep is the valley of death, great are the mountains that lye to the side. Horrors unknown to any well bred child, seen as inferior, uncivilised, ignorant, beneath even the common man, fodder for the sword and gun.

Warlock: It'sno small wonder, thatman eats man, like the lion eats the other beasts. Still the lion has been slain before the eyes of man, the vain beast who's chest pounds with pride, falters by the day. Weakened by his own weight, seeking shelter for his vanity behind the ever-decreasing boarders of his failed territories.

A joy it is to see, such failure in man, as your master decrees, his vengeance is worth a hundred thousand wars. For traitors of the spirit are in want, to spill the blood of patriots and call them in their place, reflections of action. In the house of all, lies a beast and a boar, for all their little piglets must be brought to justice by the failure of the people, their suffering and stink can be seen and heard the whole wide world over!

John: Yes, our people have taken lands before their own were taken in return, the language of their proud colonies across the seas forced upon those Picts whose gifts destroyed, destroyed our peoples in return.

The Romans served us well, providing slaves a plenty, torn from mothers' arms, fathers slain where they stood. Lines of blood, banished and scattered here and there. Now in their place our people are enslaved, yet they cry freedom as all men do.

Martin: They cry for justice, yet their penance is just, they cry beast, yet beasts their forefathers were not one thousand years before. From shore to shore our royals ruled from high above, to the western lands below, with permission from the mighty Mars, the glorious master of war, the greatest empire ever known to rule the Celts for some few hundred years or so.

Warlock: My people, my gifted flock, the dragons bright, that ruled the skies with majesty and magic wild, were taken into slavery by your rulers, many moons ago. Some go east, some go west, north and south, they walk upon the earth in life and after-life. Some to your Paradise, some stay on the earthly plane haunting the youth for thousands of years.

What price is there to pay, when wolves circle your door, drilling for the bit, a thousand years raping the earth for gold and silver, for tin and bronze, for coal and oil, for the gas of the underworld.

Now the air we breathe is poisoned when the rains come, I cannot go about myself in the bodies of living men, without them chocking or coughing with lungs fuelled by these poisonous waters.

John: Their world is crumbling, yes that's true, for prices are paid in suffering are they not? Continuation of life takes an energy that many earthy beings have, yet their appetites for stressful solutions are greater than others.

Martin: Stay the course of time, stand the waters of evil and ignorance, we shall not be moved sir and neither should you foresee the heights of the divine, for this being your domain. One or the other serves for your purpose and here shall be your eternal reward.

Neither Paradise nor Hells infernal suffering, your kind inhabit. Inside the soul of infernal fools, imbeciles, idiots and failures endless journeys. Ner-do-wells, banished and bound, confounded always the road from to Hades or Hell.

Warlock: Sounds like half of your flock, the lost souls, the people of Purgatory, the poltergeists of the frozen wastelands, the children of ignorance, masters of idiotic genius, my favourite pastime and pleasure. To find genius latent in idiotic fools, the gifted sculptor living a more humble yet fulfilling family life of the carpenter, the genius artist that paints only houses, the modern technical wizard that worked only as a labourer.

All afraid to achieve great things, fearful of what dreaming brings. One day their wooden casket brings a joyful breath of fresh air to humanity. One less baleful anti-Christ, one less baleful fool to bring suffering to the little children.

My children must suffer the full bellied beast, the fat retarded mud of idiocy and ignorance. Must suffer the beast that bullies their sensitive souls and calls them names, to destroy their souls.

John: True sir, the world is full of useless idiotic ignorant men and women. The child is disturbed by their ignorance indeed. The voices of ridicule are ever babbling in the ears and mind of the sensitive good. The well bred, educated cultured pillars of society. There's beasts of the pit beyond there and well they deserve their fate.

Martin: we cannot live in fear, for fear is an addiction that pulls the tide of curios minds into squalor and to a life of projection of blame. Many the saviour has become sinner, trying to save the devils in our midst.

In this time of great confusion, there's little merit for solutions, for everyone is selling games and profits made, fortunes for the rich, little for the impoverished.

Death has come to claim his rent, there's terror in the minds of the people. Faith has never before been sought by so many and claimed by so few.

Warlock: There's a beast amongst the pigeons, There's a cold, cold, bitter wind blowing from the north, there's a terror in the mind of the people and an army of foreign devils vying for their gold and taxes.

Whoring soullessness rules the youth, drunkenness on the streets at night beyond the pale, sacrificial lambs above and below the need for sedation from drunken nights, nothing good comes from death. Slobbing jezebels with nothing but curses flowing from their poor mouthed idolatry. Damned to be ruled by dancing demons on the roofs of the discotechs.

This is a godless world my friends, this is Hells kitchen, far and wide around the world, your people are still seen as idiots and blithering filthy imbeciles.

All I want is to rule in their place, to take back my territories of green virgin land, to reclaim my meadows, my valleys, my purified waters, my rivers and my Gods people from a foreign lands religion, its banks, its royal infidel and by your God, I will do just that!

John: They worship at the alter of nothingness, tis true. Yet born are they from stern stuff, your own agree ,far beyond the pale lie creatures baiting their breath. Lie in wait,do they the dragons of the deep, here manifest before the Seer a serpent-like creature within man, within the mind, within humanities transformation.

Here lies the truth, the blood of man, together makes enormous energies, greater than any god, greater than any devil. Mankind together rules this earth and will do so forever! (Points at Warlock with his left index finger)

Martin: Before the eyes of the Seer, before the eyes of Metatron, lies the serpent manifest, the secret of all times, a primal collective imagination. Moving through the minds and bodies of men, of children, of their mothers.

Through the Empress and the Emperor, The High and the low, transformations of spirit. Thus, the head of bodies lie, where in spirit lives and body dies.

John: Banished Goddess now headless, lost in shame, damned to infamy finds in her stead only wrath incarnate, guilt and blame. Where the ordinary being sees not the wisdom of metaphor, just entertainment for the mindless less forebrain.

Warlock: Sooth the soil `ed loins of fate, blind the minds wherein love hates.

Martin: Breath some sense into those brains, leave that life another's gains.

John: Building bridges for the damned, Jacobs Ladders found its man.

Warlock: Bitter sweet the tides of time, Open sewers rhythms of rhyme.

John: Purified the rivers free.

Martin: Glorified in victory.

Warlock: Baleful floods that cover dreams.

John: Sacred waters silver streams.

Martin: Hope for fortunes blessed times.

Warlock: Truth in fortunes victory.

Martin: You sir are not such a beast.

John: Nor saint.

Warlock: What Saint is pure, what sinner's virtue is built on strength or miracles. What God holds close where blood runs free, what lands are taken in their name, what child runs hungry from homelands state. Where God watches from above when the price of war takes its toll on the champions plate.

John: Righteous the brave and true, straight the arrow that fly's high at its target.

Martin: Mighty Jesters rule the flock, rich with fortune, women and power.

Warlock: Souls for sale on every block, desperate needs bring horrific shocks. Mountainous needs for the very wealthy, mansions high where sunsets seen. Diamond jewels and gold in stock, bonds worth their weight in a countries price. Avarice hangs their souls as Anubis weighs and measures their hearts.

To be devoured by Ammet, by The Hounds of the gate, straight down the throat, those heathen hearts all bloodied and withered with want. Power for Presidents, Kings and Queens, royals beheaded and reinstated for greed. Statesmen and Judges, Celebrities bold, whose price for their efforts paid in mountains of gold.

John: Poor mouths a plenty do sell soul and spirit for a penny.

Martin: True, a penny for sins, a penny for jealousy and drunkenness'.

Warlock: A penny for every fool, a penny for an idiot, a penny, a shilling, a shekel, a cent, a pound for the devils' little helpers. A rancid fool that follows his school of worms into the potter's ground where the filthy waters of boggy grounds drown their tired souls and strangle their last dull twinkles of hope.

Even your God offers hope to the repentant, on the death beds the most evil of them scream from fear for the lords touch. I may be ancient, but I see the light, there be peace and war in all Gods kingdoms. Murderous screams come from the mouths of many the Christian soldiers bent on the death of their enemies.Where can be seen a dual kingdom within the soul.

John: Harsh words for a harsh reality.

Martin: True, Gods warriors are the protectors of their people, for without warriors we would all be slain in our beds. Be they brave of fool alike.

Warlock: I have peace in my heart when the heavens rest their tireless slaughter of the beast within man.

John: There's a beast within us all.

Martin: That must be subdued.

Warlock: There's a powerful and mighty fearless battle-hardened warrior in the heart of every Celt, man woman and child and don't forget that! Where we fought eight thousand years, we fought ten thousand before that, and your God was nowhere but the dreams of fish and the want of badgers.

My God has been around for twenty thousand years, my priests also, the Druids, warriors all, ovates all, bards all!

Wise and strong, with a woman by their side, all beknown that your church was calling them women, selling lies and fables about blood sacrifice and that my Druids lay down with each there at night, Lies! Slander! Where your priests did unspeakable evil to the children of this race, I would drip their hearts dry and make powder of their brains! Let not those suffering evil thoughts remain in pain. For broken priest is the bain of all his countries fate.

Death and hell to those evil men! Blood and Hells whips to their souls! There are still those that do lie together with the worm and sell their shells to the children of this country and by Pit they will lie with the Devil when they die and that I know indeed.

John: Stay a while sir, we know of your anger, it is well enough.

Martin: We too are angered by the evil men, those that became evil, those that are, its true, they deserve their suffering and we good sir do not.

Warlock: Life is suffering, all congregations suffer, all animals, all gods and angels, all spirits suffer, for all of time this place is suffering and peace, life and death, day and night, male and female. Women more like men with bellowing babbling mouths and a hunger to punish the innocent child within with endless defamation of character. Men that are weak and cowardly on the inside that ruin nations and cause their offspring to fall out of grace.

Bawling loudmouthed drunken fools, that destroy their countries reputation, for the good educated flock that sacrifice their hedonism to become pillars of modern Ireland.

Idiot verses pillar, soon fulfilled it be, wise men turned to fools. Hardened swine ruled by spirits unbeknown to the innocent. Foreign devils sent from afar to balance up their judgement over long forgotten harm.

John: Tis judgement incarnate, yet hope beyond hope, these strengths in the heart of wounded warriors, wise to virtue and charity unfounded.

Martin: Those that wonder seek to find, those that take, blinded they will be, as swift as rain falls oer the ocean.

John: As hard as rockfalls from the cliff, as swift as death comes for the fallen.

Martin: There's more joy for the fool, when all has come to a fault.

Act Four

(A knock comes to the door, its Lilith again, wearing white with a red sash around her shoulder.)

John: Enter soul.

Martin: Enter spirit.

Lilith: (Enters, takes stage right, Wizard takes stage left both facing inwards towards stage centre obviously)

Lilith: Returned have I for bold in bloods eternal rivers are we, the women of death, destruction, avarice and duality.

Accountable to none, illogical to morality our ways, for driven is the soul that worships the glory of vengeance.

John: Glory to the fool that seeks sustenance in blame.

Martin: Transference of unhappy souls, the goal of hidden wisdoms revelations.

Warlock: Aye! Purpose hath the man that finds vengeance in headless quests, their aimlessness and demise.

Lilith: I see the want of evil women, not of their enemies, nor of their victims. Both evil and possessed, all of ignorance and failures rotten core. Thus reason drives the heartless horrid shameful propose of infidel and your creators fallen angels.

John: This is times immoral place. Immortal justice labouring eternally.

Martin: Thus sayeth the law. Governing injustice.

Warlock: There's blood in the body yet soul-less spirits walk the earth, husks, shells, invisible to the eyes their inner temple soon demised and despised where unwelcome hands touch in the night. This be my domain, the land of earth, the rivers left behind all dirtied and empty of life. There be few that welcome such stinking souls into their spiritual domain. Few and fewer in between.

For Gods leave well alone the fallen spirits, so bent on sin and death to fates eternal whip and scorn, there's no prayer can save the damned. Though I have seen their will alone burn an escape from the depths. A rare soul; that can indeed escape the furnace before all obstacle's.

John: Strong the will, hard to bare, ill the voices that bear false testimonies on the innocent ear.

Martin: Tall the grass that covers oer, dark the mass that buries the fallen hero.

Lilith: Sins of the parents are visited upon the children.

Warlock: Slayer of demons is the might of the slighted hand.

John: More to the point, a Christianspath is hollowed by sinful and idiotic company.

Martin: Joy of youth sworn to grief in service of truth.

Lilith: Truth allows for dominion over sinners.

Martin: By God you bore even myself and that's some feat.

John: Aye, well the evil are a boring anal lot and that's no lie.

Martin: True the devil has no qualms for sloth and boredoms his favourite meal indeed. Boredom and idiocies endless taste for ignorance and shameless acts, born from shameless fantasies.

Lilith: Well indeed its boredom leads the ignorant to my masters kingdom, for humanity has nothing but hordes of souls thrown by the wayside in search of hedonistic delights. This world offers them much to endure its hardships. Someone must deal with their uselessness, tis not your masters work, nor his angels.

True that non-believers, hypocrites and evil beings do deserve their gain along-side of self-inflicted gifts.

Warlock: I worship at the tree of temperance, I sing the praises of the ancient Gods, tis their land we tread upon and many return for their peoples destiny. Druids of my groves, masters of the elements, warrior poets, healers of all evil cancerous growths. Miracle workers, magicians of impossible feats, artist's of the veil and void, all knowing, wise to the innocent.

No Druid was ever known to harm a child, to cast them into filth for evil. Our temples did rule the earth round and still they stand in testimony six thousand years in the making.

John: True your people were banished by the sword, an injustice in the mind of our master.

Martin: Lies and dissent have been spoken about the druids, this I know to be true.

Lilith: It matters not to the evil one that druids and their Gods did rule, for evil still did hold its grip upon the ignorant misguided fool, his wife and his offspring.

Warlock: true there be fools and true their offspring suffer gladly the tidings of ignorance and idiocy, but your master did not exist in the name that you people call him, when my Gods did rule the earth. Illusion rules this modern age, where ancient Gods still rule side by side with the God of The East.

There is light and there is darkness, there is thunder and there be rain, life and death, sickness and health. There be many shades of colour for all the mind's eye to see and revel in. There be soft light and bright light, there be shadows and darkness, hearts and the heartless.

That be your domain, the land of the dead, the lifeless, the shamed and tortured.

John: Indeed The Druids of old have many stations in the afterlife, there be many more of them than there be of our own Christians. (Lilith glaring her eyes at the sound of the Christ name)

Martin: Thuss life becomes eternal thought, mind over matter, where mind is matter and matter minds the void between.

Lilith: between the void lies truth, wherefore lies infest the blind, mentality becomes more parasitical an analogy for the idiotic.

Warlock: You've got it all sorted then, you're all wise and knowledgeable. (Thy all laugh at this comment)

Fair is the race, now in its place that does blind itself with knowledge and false wisdom's analogy.

Great are the wise whose sails are set for a race of insufferable souls, good for the physical, yet infectious for the spirit.

Of this world be a bodies wide acclaim, for it's true fuel is the spirit that rules its subtle system, its magnetic light, its divine path of energy lines, binding it to the mind, itself ruled by the electrifying impulses of spirit and blood.

Spirit and blood, thought and seed, intensions flow, forgotten in the sorrows of the morrows dream.

John: By God he's right. There's a union of blood and spirit, a path only wise men follow, where blood rules appetites.

Martin: Were more than blood and spirit.

Lilith: True, your soul bodies are pure, but the living are still ruled by their bloods domain over the souls thought patterns.

Warlock: For there be a truth in your minds (Points to the saints) A truth in your lies (points to Lilith) Yet truth defined to a foolish race, leaves hidden wisdom to its other side. Blinded by the light are fools where wise-men leave no trace of deception or avarice.

Bludgeoned are the innocent and fair of faith by their fathers slighted enemies, their mothers grace destroyed by the un-tethered buffoon who's souls infested and destroyed, what a meal I make of this.

John: Your righteous rage gives hope that our Gods in his heavenly abode, for his vengeance you serve well my brother.

Martin: You're not an evil magician sir, by the sound of it you're a Godlike warrior of the druids and their Gods of thunder are served well by your purpose.

Lilith: True indeed the Good are mightier than the fallen angels and their servant's, still may I intercede that the bodies of humans fallen serve well to give sustenance and space to our lesser sprites and horned goblins. Mores the shame the whole race that's taken into my master's kingdom makes half of your species by exact number.

There's a furnace inside the soul of the fallen buffoon that serves to kindle new life until their time comes around again, if they have the wit and the will, so be it!

Warlock: Many the infernal, eternal buffoon does walk into the fires of the pit in hope your devil master will allow their God to save them from their self-inflicted addictions of failure, folly and wickedness.

A dualistic functional race does find its place in historical annals from one colony to the other. A child of goodness is tarnished as a slave when their feet tread the bloodied ground of the immeasurably tired souls that destroy their countries good name before them.

I think, they say, that I will act the fool for all the world to see, I will throw my insult bare on any given day as I do work only like ignorant soul can do, for his spirits rule in green bottled blissful slumberous wonder. My mother did born me a sensitive yet foul honourless, proud of sloth and gluttons drunken ignorance. (Dances a little jig)

John: Lies spoken by evil people, speak the truth more wisely than truth speakers.

Martin: Poetic justice.

Lilith: Reason rules where Satan squanders.

John: Jesus saves. (Lilith has a minute jaw chattering spasm, then breath's deep and sighs slowly, looking down)

Martin: Justice awaits through all lifetimes, within the hearts of the innocent, lie demons of great evil awaiting the vengeance of the fool, the imbecilic, the horrific monster's of alcoholism and the underprivileged.

Warlock: The underprivileged do indeed need to vilify the privileged, for do the privileged not outshine their hard, heartlessness with sensitivity and grace? Who's heart is not set upon by the poor mouth child? Who's head is not destroyed by the demons of the rejected? What graceful virgin is not despised by the jealous unkempt underdogs of blame?

Burning at the spires of shame, lie the broken bodies of the innocent, who's thoughts are seen as diseased by the hard-hearted children of ignorant parents, of forlorn godlessness and envy? History has long forgotten the actions of foreign devils, dark hearted souls thirsty for death and slavery for the soft and gentle children of well-bred privileged Christian homes?

John: Tis the hunger for equality.

Martin: The new religion of the obsessed.

Lilith: The child of the underprivileged works well for my master, suffering and blame leaves nothing to the afflicted, damned to blame, damned to shame and damned to take the lives of their enemies that live up onhigh. How effortlessly they feel judged, how ruled by envy are they, how easily swayed to serve the gods of evil and of ignorance, how ugly the soul that lies in wait to equalise the child of innocence.

How too the spoiled child from godless parents does see the light of innocence laying within their own glorified superiority. The child of empire,Satan's flock, the great genocidal hunger of the royals of old, the soulessness of modernity, the endless hunger for power that the child of the innocent serves to create.

John: Leading the innocent into Hell, is the path of the imbecile.

Martin: Leading the children into Hell, leave the imbecile here in place of his spirits last domain.

Warlock: yes, here in my kingdom, where life and death do meet, the spirits of the dead do dwell, unwelcome in paradise, unwelcome in Hell. For by serving both sides, by leading others into failure, the spirits of the damned do haunt the shadows for eternal lifetimes. Cold-hearted weak-willed bastards, (Looks to audience) pardon my French, deserve to suffer endlessly, yet our own living still suffer the cold unwelcome hands of the sick dead stinking moronic fools that lie in dark corners awaiting their rebirth by some trick of destiny.

John: There's always an out.

Martin: By the crow flies, there's always an escape, though it be a road of infinite impossibilities.

Lilith: Heartless instead of empty hearted, soulless instead of spiritless, meaninglessness instead of mercilessness, hardship within leas to hardship without. Subjugation, colonisation, more Philistines and glorious empire laid bare.

Taxing, charging, punishing, imprisoning, banishing, breaking their will, taking their self-respect and drowning them to the mix. Speaking ill of them, wasting their strength, selling them addictions, prostituting them, wining and dining on their bare and broken backs.

Warlock: Taking theirs and all they hold dear, giving only wilderness and boggy grounded wastelands, forcing slavery to foreign lands. There's the man that climbs out of Hells doubling troubling struggling lands. Kings made to beggars and beggars to kings. Queens killing children and taxing the people for the cost.

The devil doesn't ruin this world all on his own, he has the nonbelievers and the insane religious hypocrites to do his bidding. For pagan and Christians did battle long and hard for their little piece of stone.

John: Over the hill and far away, the children of innocence fear little of what has been before. You would scare them in their beds with stories of the Devils and his hell. Surethere's a paradise to end all suffering, lakes of pure waters to cleanse all souls eternal suffering. Golden angels of almighty brightness to blind the illusions of this world and the next.

Martin: All that is seen and unseen, all that is holy and unholy, all that is truth and all that lies. All that is wrong, all that fears, all that causes fear, all that hates, all that endues hatred.

John: All that empowers, all that destroys, all that gives life, all that takes life, all of Gods children living strong, all that are weak, all that worship at the feet of the ignorant.

Lilith: All that wear the clothes of the priests, all that are whipped by the rules from the east. All that is unseen, obscene, all that lies and lives with deceit. The embarrassment of those who's inner beauty hath vanished, been banished. The men that are more women than men, the women that are more men than women, all demand to be feared. All demand to recruit the youth.

These beings serve my master well, though their loins be ruled by shame, though their souls recover not, though their families suffer for their sin. They seem to care not, even when compassion rolls down their faces, imbeciles damn themselves and all around them damn their names.

Warlock: The hypocrites become saints, the saints hypocrites, the sinners find salvation the religious fall to hell. There's the rub indeed my friends there's no easy road from this here place and that's for sure.

Though they defecate in their clothes, their filth lies more where ere they lie, where ere they walk their residue leaves a stink behind. Their appetites blind their pain, there's a thirst for hedonism that's beyond their working weeks end. There's brimstone and hell fires burning bright for the souls of sinfulness and hedonistic delight. No God nor Devil wants those helpless sinners, serving the prey their sins away, then tongue the foul stench of lies and need again. Till beauty becomes beast and stench cannot be quenched by perfume nor bathing.

John: You both paint a bleak picture.

Martin: We hear you sir, everyone in this audience hears you(He motions across the audience with his right hand in a sweeping motion)

They all have suffered within confined restriction. We all know of death and of life, we know of vanity, greed and ignorance. We live in a world controlled by thought alone, by action, word and gesture, by slight and might, by deed, greed and need.

By a mothers soothing hand, by a drunken slobbering beast, by the wisdom of a kind word, by the slanderous lecherous damned. For one life as an idiot, another as an oxen laden with the burden of servitude.

Liliith: Taking hard hearted beings into the Shibin, into the underworld, where only the rejected can be found. There lies a debt that can never be repaid, doctors, fathers, mothers, lawyers, judges, warriors bold and beauties bound to repay their lord and masters.

There's a hanging tree that's lies outside the brookby the river, there down by the cottages white and the palaces grand. The bloodied gowns of broken souls by the slight of evil are they damned.

Warlock: Poetess (He nods his head in approval-the two saints exchange glances of "Could there be hope of reform?") By the by, we hear your painful cries and true agreed we do see there's a desire for justice within the slighted heart. The wounded pride, the imprisoned paupers, the hungered soul with a fearless thirst for the life of their royal enemies.

There indeed lies a darkened heart in every home, a wise hand that holds the blade, a brave heart that forgives all enemies. For I have seen all enemies go down, swift and easy, all contenders fall to sloth and slumber, all slighted hearts receive mercy and justice when they forgive. The price for freedom lies in the truth and the truth is as all secretive sins, as simple as can be.

John: Well said sir.

Martin: Here here!

Lilith: Where lies the great man, I do agree, there lies no fame nor vanity. Riches a given to his family, to charitable acts and philanthropy. This man my servants cannot touch, cannot whip nor scorn, now do we stay his place, nor have a taste for his thoughts or words. They serve to sting and smite our souls. Its true, there's only hatred in my heart, but the love of hatred drives me on to serve the people that serve me in return.

Their blood boils and pours at every corner, their chemistries fuel the fires of suffering and pain. There's is selfishness and fear, ignorance and blame. Yet they still serve your master on the other foot and this is why they enter not your masters kingdom, nor mine.

We cannot have screams for God in Hell, nor the thirst for sin in the other place, that's your domain.

John: True indeed there's a fool on every corner that serves a subtle insufferable idiocy and ignorance.

Martin: The faces that scare children and ridicule the young are more enough than guilty of sin and ignorance.

Warlock: A wonderful world it is, where idiots rule, donkey headed imbeciles bent over double with their backside reared to the world like whores for the beast. There's a reputation known around the world for many the fool lies dormant as empty vessels in waiting.The pigs behind seeks only cruelty, the punished mouth of the brutish swine, the pain their spirit brings into the home. This wondrous shell does find life's purpose in meddling with innocence, judging of the free hedonistic youth experimenting with life's flexible boundaries.

John: Boundaries are another of my master's rules.

Martin: Broken rules bound for those without a clue.

Lilith: Breaking promises lead not the path of the righteous, broken souls come this way and far greater the soul that's broken is the shame they bring their country, their family and their endless servitude to disgrace.

Warlock: Harsh your world must be, harsh the suffering of the people born unto this world. Strong the soul that's equal to its spirit, endless the warriors fearless and honoured in victory. Boundless abandon through thick skinned wearied knights, thankless tasks, unrecognised achievements, strength in numbers mindless bravery.

John: True brave souls that falter not in war are reared by the Lord above (Lilith takes a panicked breath, with a deep look of distain) Killing foreign foe has no debt nor punishment. Thankless tasks are well received by the spirit if not by the people they serve.

Martin: Concerned pillars of society extraordinary situations marked the whole, scared the people that live lowly, the rich in spirit whose lives are marred and smeared by the fools next door. There lies the rub, there a better life to be had, against the grain of jealous ignorance. Yet ambitions hunger holds no quarter for environment, for consequence.

Liliith: Defeat holds pure the dream of ashes, exhausted souls bear fruit to the joy of vanity, the love of suffering, of destruction. It's a great taste of pleasure for all evil beings, for the ignorant masses, for the fools next door to the pillars that serve your Master.

Warlock: Soundless hoards floundering wavelike into the bowels of the pit, yes indeed an eternal river of suffering for all comers. Hitherto this world is not made for such things, as great as the Gods are, their lands are blessed by spirits grand.

John: True sir! Indeed, your words are received with warmth and gladness.

Martin:Aye, there's a blessing in the old Gods and well they have been ignored by the followers of the new.

Lilith: (Looking annoyed at the three male characters singing praises to Gods old and new)There's riches untold for any man that worships my lord.

Warlock: Those riches are not his to give, the Goddess holds sway over all jewels and precious metals. Tis the warden of Hell that's your master, his heart lies bound in great glaciers beneath, his tears limitless and within his empty heart lies endless grief.

Martin: True indeed, The Devils lair is a far cry from Earthly Paradise.

John: A prison for tortured souls.

Lilith: Well for them that follow evil. Know they little of consequence, your words ring not on the deaf, nor can the blind see your light, more so those that can, eat well from both black and from white.

Warlock: Truth from the mouth of evil is rare indeed. Till the mountains crumble the gods of old rule supreme over this fair kingdom. The Goddess of the rivers wide, the oceans deep, the stream, the sacred springs. Old Brigit of Irelands gentle lands that cure the blind and feed the soul with silver light beyond all ailments is truly blessed.

John: We did Christianise those same spring Saints.

Warlock: True your lands are baptised by a foreign God and he holds sway over all. But the old Gods favour nature and natures religions are returning. There be some here amongst us that worship now the ancient ways, their laws are saving nature right before the eyes of evil. A terrible disease that many under you fathers rule destroyed this Earthly Paradise like blinded fools. Gold, gold and precious jewels from blood.

Martin: Lessons learned, we are leaving those dark days behind us, the rivers are now finding health again. Things change slowly after destruction.

Lilith: Gone are the days of spiralling expansion, holding strong to the ways of revenge and blame. Ragged thorns await the children of your master, imps and lesser demons rule upon their dreams. Slick the cold hearted fallen angels, building webs for the waste of the unborn.

Warlock: Your a barrel of laughs you are! My Gods rage war on your master and your tongue! Great are the beasts of the field and all unknown leviathans. Down to the pit for all eternities whirling wheels of busted war and infestation, strong is the magic of the Druids, for ther one eyed one rules over all! (He casts his staff at the floor of Lilith, a blast of smoke is let off at her feet, along with the sound of thunder and a flash of lightening on the back stage screen.)

(Lilith cowers down to the stage floor in fear until the pandemonium passes)

John: Well done sir.

Martin: Here here.

Lilith: (Showing reverence) I am a part of the human race sir, I ask not for forgiveness, nor reprieve. I too have suffered the sloth of the sinful hedonistic slobbish hoards in my lifetime, seen fates cruel hand awaiting and lingering on the shores of the fallen. I understand vengeance, I absolve evil, I forgive lusts and greed unknown to the good people. My world is of shame, of blame and guilt, my damnation is to hold the cup of sin within my soul. All purities of Mankind are seen to rot the marrow of chastity and faith. All charities banished by the hands of infidel and imbecilic. There's a level in Hell for all fallen beings. There's a special place for those possessed, for those that practice evil magic, for those that take what is not theirs.

Warlock: Your tongue is surely gifted for your path is well drawn, the path for fallen hero's and heroin's. The waters of putrid blackness and rot run true and eternal into the pit. Tis true there's still a heart though within even the average faultless fool, for all pleasures, for all the chemistries of want lead down and emptied vessels true.

John: The dove hath claws, the mothers of the innocent have strength unbound and fearless in the face of peril or beast are they in defence of their child.

Martin: The ever moaning evil baleful chastising imbecilic being, who's souls diseased, finds little patience with protectors, close to taking vengeance on their heads.

Lilith: Your judgement of my world is true, still someone must provide a space, where rotten apples end their days. No cold cavernous earthly plane makes room for the damned eternal soul. For moments yes, they haunt their watery graves, their scatted ashes serve nothing, no worm, no raven, no maggots are appeased by their last sacrifice to this world nor the next.

Warlock True the poetess of the macabre are you, I think there's hope yet you'll serve my Gods some day. They have little regard for evil men, their vengeance heavy, their sword swift, no reprieve, nor salvation has the dark goddess for wicked women, nor evil men. There be swine ungraceful, grievous will, possessed by devils, imps and lesser demons in this world, many of whom wear the cloth of the preacher. Reprieve for damned sickening swine does not exist, not on their death beds nor in Hell neither.

John: Yes, perhaps we have been too stern with you(Motions towards (Lilith)

Warlock: It would be few that lye on mountain rocks, that slave to drive all artistries out, all giant gifts that they do mock, must serve to damn their souls in stead. More sensitive hands that dwell in Paradise, did suffer grand in this here life, by thoughts unknown from jealous rivals, whose art exposed if only to terrorise.

Lilith: Yes, the slaves of vanity reversed are truly obsessed with the creations of sensitive souls, those you call angels by their nature alone. I myself have grace, I myself am served by lowly sickening fallen beings, yet I create genius reversed, paintings grand to please the damned, music soothing for my masters ears, written into the pacts so many make with his servants' up above on Terra Firma.

John: True your wishes do come true for those that sell their souls and make pacts for fame and fortunes fleeting place. Gold and good names bought and sold, lifetimes of world renown, fame and power. Handed down by your master for a coin, for a word, a deed for a deal.

Martin: There be few if any on the earthly plane that acquired fame without such things, so few and scarce and far between. Our master allows only the disciplined to sing his praises and capture his kingdom for all his grand temples of this world.

Lilith: I have child, I know of love, of innocence within the dark hearted ones. True pure a heart of darkness, it holds firm the pleasure of its purpose what my kingdom holds in its heart, though it be one of opposing truths to yours. It must exist, it must derive its price from failures and hypocrites, for they also must reside in their soulless castles, hard won by sin and want and greed. Long lives of excess, riches untold, power, glory, fame and fortune, tis one reason why the platform exists for such things. As above so also below.

Warlock: Well we know of pacts and deals, for this worlds full of those that signed in blood those very same deeds. Our greatest poets and bards from long ago. The world-wide fame and power of the rich and famous, the artists whose souls sold out and, in their pictures, lie the vacuums left in their wake. There be wanton fools that break all rules, have crafts beyond the bold and true. There be sinners in Paradise forgiven wide and saints in Hell for their art and for their poetry that's hard to see fault in.

John: Yet fault therein lies, within the oils of humanities greatest works, within the vowels of their greatest songsters and writers, all subtle secrets, hidden messages, subliminal and obvious to the senses.

Martin: Yet therein lies the obvious, to well worn eyes, to the wise mind, the experienced hand, the true of heart, the quick before the dead. Useless souls block thy path, ugly morbid imbeciles, born of ignorance and addiction.

Lilith: Though I see truth still, as the mocking songster, the drunken painter, the idolised poet. All masters of the absolute, obsessed with sex and death. Fear and foolishness, abandoned by their lord, rejected by their fickle flock. The solitude of fame, takes its toll of their gifted genius and talented souls.

Warlock: Aye indeed, there's a must and need to place the true genius into their fallen place. Tis obvious to me at least, what lies beneath the cosmic lover's skin. There's a face that needs to hide its true colours. Still tis earth gives some rest to famous souls, their work is an art all of its own. Especially where it gives hope to the good and the true that are innocent.

John: Yes, martyrs mend their efforts well and serve humanity with great works expelled as exorcism's of their pain.

Martin: Remedies lost to addiction and scorn, well the bards must sell their own.

Lilith: They sell their soul and do pact with the master beneath. His powers control all powerful and wealthy, all subtle sins, all songs of love, all painting sold for millions, where their creators died penniless and alone. There's a beauty in the beast, a music there from old, where Pans Labyrinths do grace that muse for all that genius men hold dear, for recognition, for money, fame and also repetition.

Warlock: All the world is round, all dreams become ambitions, all wants to will, all needs fulfilled, ahh the sound of beauty from a beast, from handsome thwarted artistry. How close to Paradise they are until their bellies growl empty, when thirst defeats and rejection destroys all remnant's of humanity. Tis then the angels fall, the man does cry enough, the woman too gives up and selling souls comes easy.

John: What of this world you do not know? What of Gods children (Lilith holds her hands over her ears for a second) One hand of the scale's goes high, the other low, one lives, one dies, one casts a spell for the whole world over, the other in obscurity does thunder from their afterlife to rule supreme and immortal.

Martin: For all illusions, miracles a plenty, fallen angels artistry does tell lies to the mind. The Wizardry of suffering hides its secrets from the eyes of the people. But the eyes of the wise, see through all evil. Theres suffering in art painted by the soul in peril that only the wise can see.

Lilith: Yes indeed, for much more gold is bought and sold to the people by the clever minded and the greedy. What of lies dressed all in silver, what of stories sold as truths, of miracles, of fortuitous favours given to the chosen few. Beast dressed as beauty, lapis lazuli crushed with gold, slivered on the canvas in beautiful blue hues, spiralling waves of colour in starry skies. With golden dreams and promises of dreams coming true, of opiates within the mind designed to lessen fear and pain. (She dances a little, gracefully) What of ochre's, incense and of pleasures, beatitudes of abandon and of leisure. For many the soul that has tried to find your masters grace has also fallen out of it by worshipping both light and dark, tis in their art, al hidden and merged together as two snakes wrapped in each others embrace.

Warlock: My, my, your beauty blinds the senses (Lilith motions a subtle smile) Still a devils adevil all the same, no offence to their credence. There's work to be done in that there domain we above don't wish to serve. There's infested souls here that no child deserves to suffer. On any given day that man is told, Eve is the route of evil. Yet men then are blamed for all evil.

There's a special rotten place in Hell for both men and women. For a lifetime's evil done to children of all ages. The less of hurt, the more of blame, the addicts cause projects its name, upon the heads of all that prove their worthless horrific face, with melted skin more like disease.

John: Yes sir, its true, there's no place for a devil than its human vessel, living or in the cold spirit body here high or low. Here there be dragons and beasts far greater than any spirit world.

Martin: Shame on humanity, shame on all of us.

Lilith: No need to get so down, after all, there's a joy in judgement is there not. Evils path is eternal, as your path is, one for the other as the weather, as the waters and the bridges that cross over them. For every damaged child there's one that shines. I myself know whom I serve, yet my castle is grand, my servants crystal clear and pure as the driven snow. Secretaries of the damned.

There are riches untold for those illuminated by the light of the fallen angel. We choose our destinies, we overcome all obstacle's as your master well knows he himself did also. Yes my gold is won from war, from rich men as from poor. Yet all gold comes from suffering. I must worship rules also. I must see only rewards in dominion, as a queen of mankind as the punisher also of women, unaccountable and unreasonable as they think they are. There's a special place in Hell for fallen women. For great is the suffering they cause, great their ignorance and shame, their hypocrisy, their immaturity, their aggression and insult flowing deep into obsession.

Warlock: Of this Im sure. No greater fear do mothers have than of ignorant and evil women. The child sent off to school must learn of vengeance, or jealousies' grand, or vain pleasures lost when the ghosts of their possessed enemies fall on them with subtleness unforeseen.

John: What rage I feel for evil then, when it suffers great hurt for deeds so repugnant and reviled.

Martin: What piteous relief when the evil are bound by the warlocks and magicians, for this work also is not of (pauses to look at Lilith, knowing if he says God, she will cringe) my master.

Lilith: I too once served your lord, long ago before my tribe wasted by invading hoards did be. My innocent to slaughter, my precious lands laid waste. All language banned, all music, all mythologies caused to illegality. My golden haired daughters destroyed by the sword, then forced to live as slaves, worse than slaves. In grassless pits with rags and poverty unknown to animals, with raging parents damned to alcoholism and eternal shame.

Famine and plague driven deep within the soul, the mind its own enemy, the beast within grown rancid till its shell becomes diamond hard. There's the birthplace of demons great, with one dream only, vengeance and revenge.

Warlock: Your bringing tears to my eye's woman.

John: Tis your place then to deliver vengeance, though scripture's say otherwise.

Martin: The only mystery in suffering and death is of its true source, that is not of my master, true that scripture says otherwise.

Lilith: Paradise returns to the lord of light, when his penitence is up, when his vengeance has ended, when all life has stopped and all Suns return to nothing. And all the deserts dust, all oceans emptied, all precious life dissolved and origins resolved.

An angry man or woman is likened to the beast, for anger is the master of evil things. I don't sup on poisoned berries, I drink the nectar of health, I walk up and down on these fair lands as I please. This world and all its beauty, all that I see before me is mine. No God takes that from me. Tis just my place to oversee the fallen`s place, for your master holds no sway over them.

Warlock: Weakened spirits, soullessness and haste, fatherless children left to their mothers' hatred of the same. Tis indeed an ugly world full of ugly people. There's the child of reason that makes an army of his chosen path. There's the hand that feeds all mouths, good, ill, or ignorant. For the beast within eats well its fill from the garden.

The child that comes from suffering can become the master of sufferings cause and make his fortune healing others. Oblivious to health as many souls are, there's wealth in goodness and a keen eye needed to avoid its rival.

John: Solid sound spirits woe, righteous beings sold to suffering, when strength was sold and fortunes bound without reason. Stomachs virtue lies in temperance, livers lie not to the death of healthy bodies. Spirits within those same fallen people see the light when the innocent bless their paths.

Martin: Harsh hounds calling forth from their slumber, bate the heels of all living beings. Bright minded youth found floundering at wits-end for less than small favours or interests. Roaring beasts of the field working the city streets calling forth for vengeance and revenge, marching out for death and glory on golden headed heroes and heroin's.

Lilith: Truth be told, that pillars crumble and high heads topple, rivers run dry and valleys perish into dust. Yet there be a place in each lifetime for even a devil to enter Paradise. For many have done so when their reflections cease for evils path. Not without endlessness, eternal suffering and pain first of course, you can beat a fool to become anything but a fool.

Whose voice they hear roaring high and then call cease, stop enough. For whom the winding path to Hell has no end in sight, is eternal and offers still escape for all-comers lost within. The beast lies on that last stopping post a-waiting fools and jokers alike, some that value their wits over his. There have been a few whose perilous spirits have passed his staff and found their escape to the halls of Purgatory.

Warlock: Therein those golden lacquered halls, there's a calling for great appetites, for shamelessness and evils unknown to most good people. For power makes Gods of men and of women. Palaces standing still to men's eyes give countenance to vanity and glorious costumes that only a well-bred, respectful lady should wear.

Taken from the eastern fields, slaves and prostitutes unkempt have now returned for to eat their fill, to spend all taxes, to live in homes built for the people. The law of give and take rules upon the heads of all and nowhere is sanctuary from the foreign devil's unquenchable thirst and hunger. Tax payers now the slave, governments the master, restlessness rules all cities, banished are the peoples promises of rewards. Bless them all, my little piglets.

John: This world gives enough and little more.

Martin: Enough rewards for the educated child, for whom without, who would heard the lamb, or the pup?

Lilith: There's a place for the innocent, if innocent their forefathers and mothers be. My master cannot touch the head of an unblemished mind, nor whisper in the ears of the virgin white, nor the truly gentle soul. There's a hundred thousand living here who's lives are visited by calamity. Yet their strengths being tested leave only vacant memories of blame, not landing on their shoulders but on their vengeful enemies. Yet scarred anyone can be for slights and slanderous comments, tis the way of things as well you know.

I have an eye for beauty still that's beyond the greatest mind until as time goes by, beauty vanishes. Yet beauty within shines out as brightly as the new-born child, I cannot lie and paint all humanity as ugly or putrid. There's a foul tale being told of my true place in this world; indeed all have dualistic sides, all have darkness, all have good. Day and night both have precious jewels in their crowns, do they not? (Holds her hands out palms up)

Warlock: In the absolute indeed there's a place for all and all dualistic natures agreed in type do send their children out into the world. Both good and evil, sensitive and ignorant. One rule fits all, some stand, some fall. There's the rub where weakness grows in some, strength does so in others.

Although to blame those accustomed to the darkness for weaknesses in mankind is a dangerous game. For the saints in Hell that fell into disgrace, astounded are we that see truly evil men baptised by the light, forgiven and rising to the divine.

John: No rules will deny that sir.

Martin: Music soothes the soul and anger destroys the innocent when tested they be.

Lilith: There's a trance out hypnotic sound that rules the minds of gifted artists, those that make pacts with my master and hold the Universe in their hands. All that they see before them, all powers hold over the imbecilic clowns and jokers that dance their death dance around the minds of your innocent youth.

Your innocent youth brought down to Hell by the Ravens of Death, the spirits of unhappy souls, bound to the earth plane, whose voices ridicule the living and rule the minds of bullies, cowards and abusers.

Warlock: This be the work of the earth-bound souls, this be a place where all elementals abide, beneath the earth, on the earth, in the waters and the winds above. For all damned souls must be cast from heaven and from Hell. The cackling voices of the evil and the imbecilic ignorant. They live amongst us, they ruin our thoughts, they destroy our governing druids, they invite in foreign powers, Gods and Kings to rule upon their own heads. What damned fools live here? Where do the good escape such a world? One son berates another, one mother bates some others with serpent tongued distain, one sin upon the other grows like weeds in the fields.

There's a place for justice and those that seek revenge, nor are they welcome in any home nor in any body they possess. Old, young or otherwise.

John: This is the time of angels, there is a ladder rising forth above man and his beasts. There are angels all around us now gaining in strength, throwing their message around for all to see. Secrets to astound the mind, shared by fellow friends and spirits unknown.

Martin: Artistic creations for the everyman, just to illuminate the glorious day, free up the soul and body from life's stresses and build constant reminders towards the higher levels.

Lilith: There's a path that rises above, Ill agree with that and that's the journey for the brighter minds, the good, the innocent and the hard fought, ever struggling people. The long suffering ones whose philanthropic hearts survive the diabolical never-ceasing onslaught the imbecilic servants of idiocy and evil deliver to their doors.There's no denial that goodness exists, it's just the people responsible for destroying it that think they have goodness themselves. Giving birth to ignorance, thus the ignorant spirit is banned from both spheres and is bound to this one.

Such is my sides meaning of life, in taking, or trying to take all goodness that offends the hearts and minds of idiots and evil beings away, does that souls reward be eternal haunting of the living be . There's the cold hearted hand that reaches out to touch the sleeping child, to whiten the hair of the youth before their time, to terrify the innocent on a dark and wintery storms sleepless night.

Warlock: There's the rub! (Starts to walk about all the characters and takes the stage more than usual) Revel in the damned that dwell in shadows and in dark forgotten places. Their drunken souls now all about this changing world of many faces. From all around the sphere they come, all suffering, all baleful, all victims of great empires and the fools that serve for a penny and for a sliver of self respect. Once Royalty, now pauper, once pauper now royalty. Old gold new, new gold old. Saint to Sinner, Sinner to Saint. Genie of prostitute, innocence thrown to blind sights set on pleasures born of natural opium's and blood.

This country did indeed serve its people up as servants to their own miserable soulless inhuman devil's master. To make martyrs of their name, for to live here ever-after as punishment for the same! What does a soul want that's bound to the shadows of this world for an eternity? It seeks revenge, it seeks vengeance on the children of its enemies, the slighted hand, the word that brings an end, the sinful act unpunished leads to punishment again.

John: Yes, still this world is all illusion, there's a place even for the souls bound to the shadows, for this be their time to enter the light. This be the time that comes every thousand years for all souls, living and dead to enter the light divine, here on this plane and in the next. Jacobs Ladder, hidden to all yet seen by the many.

Martin:Of this fair world there's more be spoken of and of each man there be a tale, of each sinful path a reason and a gift in toe. A space for salvation, a mark from what's taken or given in repose.

Lilith: A marked and creviced lined palm and bloodline, true, there's music in the underworld that soothes the tired soul, this great and woven place and palace is for the pleasures of the body. Even your own sweet selves have delved into the tastes for women in your youth before your sainthood. Again in the turn of the tides mankind does still have its innocents. I am not your enemy good sirs, I avail for the given greed of fools, as your kings do for the safety of their people.

Warlock: Yes well, for your kingdom I indeed have seen is guarded and guided by the hounds of the gates, thus far have I gone and no further. For those lands beneath are of my lords and deities also. Each has a mind of alternate beliefs and all structures represented therein seem opposite and alternate in their guises. There's no Pan in our arboreal worlds, no Thor, no Ra, nor great spirits from far away places. Just ancient deities awaiting their children's return to the underworld of illusion, shell without soul, or spirit, slaves to their compulsions, their addictions, their appetite's for energies outside of their own. Some call it animal, some anima-animus in modern mental healers hands. The cold land of the dead ghosts is a safer place to be, thus this world has its fill of secluded souls.

Thus the sights seen and unseen can only be the ancient ones. Not one Christian dies this day that sees what he thinks he will see. Yet all that's seen will be what his elders know for the last fifteen hundred years or so. There's no conversions in the light, there's all but one and another sight to see. All seeing eyes of Gods known and unknown. Gods of purpose and goodness, of peace and bliss, thus such a state reflects that beneath, as all things do, for every demonic soul, an angelic one, though Sunshine days are recollected far easier by the good and rain come quick by the will of evil and ignorant people. Gods bless us.

All equal, all divine, all benevolent, all powerful and wise.

John: What world is this? Your tongues now sweet and divine, surely your world is of natures spirits. We judge you swift and forgiveness is in order. (Wizard salutes him respectfully) For where's

90

the hope without natures spirits? Where's the sanity? Where's the power of my lord? Says the everyman, yet where's the strength of his conviction? Of for womankind, of her belief? Where their youthful beauty lies destroyed, all that's left is strength restored. Strength that was beaten out of them by life's eternal suffering, life's hard learned and painful lessons. Recovered by miracles and faith in higher powers whatever Gods they follow.

Roaring to my God, my father, my master andall knowing for pity and mercy on their broken lives. Known and unknown the thoughts, actions and deeds of undecidedfaceless fools.

Martin: Well said sir, though my lord is a forgiving God, his divine chaste mother all compassionate, the souls of suffering do not listen to their conscience, have no sound nor tastes for others, nor taste for others grief. Their ignorance unbounding, their hearts possessed by grief.

Well in another lifetime, their sins destroy all dreams, their offspring cast aside beneath the trodding feet of ignorance and greed. Their cries for help unheard, their countries built for foreign hoards, this world is made a Paradise yet some can only come and go like tumble-weeds through the desert.

Lilith: Well the wisdom of life balances all things, all weather-worn mountains ancient where once tall spiked summit's ley. Still the glory of kings and queens falls into the dust, all heroes and heroin's but in their name alone, in their deeds brave and valiant. Left to the side in their old age many of them.

Warlock: Aye, but the spirit lives eternal, there's the rub in folklore and song, poetry and tale of wise and powerful beings become Gods themselves by the grace of The Almighty Lugh, by the hand of The Dagda, by Slough Fegs horns and Brigit's grace men become their Gods in spiritual ways manifested.

John: This be true sir. Yet all Gods fail mankind, all diseases overwhelm all cultures, where's the power of your Gods them, or my

God, may he be appeased at my theosophical mind.

Martin: yes, all Gods fail mankind, although mankind now has become overseer for ailments. God also performs miracles for some and none for others, this is the way of things.

Warlock: True enough my Master's are worshipped by the children of Crom, the black Worm. Thusmodern and ancient dogma mirror the same prophesies that life is suffering. That disease overwhelms all true believers and non believer's alike.

I know well all religion is illusion, all Gods made manifest by their counterparts here on Earth. Angelsflight divine light and all falls asunder by the by. Hards the road, high the hill deep the valley, quick the waters flow. Here-gone, birth to swan-song, war and peace gentle being to beast. One takes another, one gives charity all throughout their life, one kills the other, one takes their own life.

Lilith: Hard is the road, many saints fallen, many wondering why their master ignores their pain, their suffering and still the clouds gather, the rain falls eternal, the good die young, the saintly fall, the animal's rule in their place. Mother nature watches all, in days gone by she took them swiftly, by hard heated weather your people did not live long, nor did they have much time to sleep. Now that modernity gives some respite, one hundred years has passed and all that they hold dear is falling through their fingers.

John: Hards the road that we survive.

Martin: That our people suffer and reveal.

Warlock: True the deed of life is hard yet soft too in equal measure.

Lilith: In equal opposition-opposing equalities.

John: Opposing equalities of equal measure justified in balance.

Martin: Opposing balances carried by angelic justice.

Lilith: Justice the cruel merciless and exact.

John: Exact in measure.

Martin: Freedom and death.

Warlock: Both opposing opposites.

John: Thus the tear of the innocent leads to the pain and punishment of the evil.

Martin: Thus the attempt of evil is also thwarted.

Warlock: Freedom for the enslaved.

Lilith: Enslavement for the innocent.

John: As above.

Martin: So below

Warlock: As above.

Lilith: So below:

The End

Printed in Great Britain
by Amazon

54600813R00058